I Had a Best Friend Too

CA Pranav Sharma

ISBN
Paperback 979-8-89906-266-7
Hardcase 979-8-89929-701-4

DEDICATION

Parents are the reason for our existence. Hence, this book is dedicated to my Parents. Without their relentless support, this book would not have been completed.

ACKNOWLEDGMENT

Writing a book is often a solitary endeavor, but finishing one is always a collective effort. This book exists not just because I wrote it, but because of the many hands, minds, and hearts that helped shape it along the way.

To the readers—who pick up stories and give them life beyond the page. Your support means everything.

To my mentors and teachers—Ms. Sharda Madam and Ms. Preeti Madam—who instilled in me a love for storytelling. Their influence lingers in every word I write.

To my wife, Ms. Annapurna Sharma, my toughest critic and greatest supporter. Her patience and insight shaped this book in ways words cannot fully express.

To my family and friends—who encouraged, motivated, and occasionally forced me to take breaks when I got lost in my words.

A book, once written, belongs to its readers. I hope this story stays with you long after the last page is turned.

With gratitude,

CA Pranav Sharma

CHAPTER 1

August, 2009

It was 6 a.m.—to begin with. The New Delhi railway station was already astir. Tea vendors shouted their wares, their kettles hissing like restless serpents. Coolies, clad in faded uniforms and red turbans, wove through the crowd with practiced ease, hoisting trunks and suitcases as if they weighed nothing. Passengers hurried along, some glancing at their watches, others peering at reservation charts with furrowed brows. The air carried the mingled scents of chai, sizzling snacks, damp newspapers, and iron tracks. A voice crackled over the speakers, droning about train arrivals and departures, but few paid any heed.

The frequent announcement —"May I have your attention please..." made the passengers quicken their steps, to board their train before it departed.

Pranav stood outside Shatabdi Coach C-8, the morning air cool against his face, as he leaned closer to the printed reservation chart. His eyes scanned the list until they stopped at a familiar name: 'Aparna Mishra.' He smiled.

Train charts, printed and pasted beside the coach door, were once reliable sources of surprises. In the days before apps and algorithms, a journey's true companions were often revealed by ink on paper. And there it was—

Seat No: 58 | Name: Aparna Mishra | Age: 24 | Gender: F

Right beside his own.

He stepped back and adjusted the strap of his bag, the faint memory of childhood summers stirring somewhere deep within him. The train, meanwhile, waited patiently, its wheels humming with quiet anticipation as though it, too, sensed the reunion in the making.

The coach had exactly seventy-eight seats, arranged in a disciplined 3x2 fashion—three on one side, two on the other—repeating with unwavering regularity. But, like all things in life, there were exceptions. The first and last rows, for reasons best known to railway planners, had been granted a special 2x2 arrangement, as if to set them apart from the rest.

He did a quick mental calculation. "Seats 58 and 59 should be together. Fate has been kind today," he mused before stepping aboard.

Pranav hesitated at the doorway, gripping the strap of his bag. A strange stillness settled in his chest, like the quiet pause before a storm. He inhaled slowly, steadying himself before stepping inside.

Inside, Aparna sat by the window, her chin propped on her palm as she gazed outside, absorbed in thought. A deep blue Kurti wrapped around her frame, its fabric catching the soft glow of morning light. Gold earrings glinted each time she shifted, reflecting fleeting sparks of brightness—like fireflies in motion... Her rimless spectacles rested lightly on her nose, an unassuming barrier between her and the world. He told himself they kept him safe, protecting him from drifting too far, from losing himself in depths he could never return from. Yet, a quiet thought lingered— if the spectacles were to slip, even for a moment, would he be able to resist the pull?

Pranav hesitated for a moment before taking the seat beside her.

There was something about her—something that tickled the edges of Pranav's memory, like a tune half-remembered.

"Good morning," she said, her voice calm, detached.

"Morning. Looks like we are travel companions," he replied, lowering himself into his seat.

She nodded. "So, it seems."

A blaring horn pierced the air as the train departed right on schedule—6:20 a.m.

The train rumbled forward, leaving the city behind. Inside the compartment, the rhythmic clatter of wheels, the rustle of newspapers, and the occasional murmur of conversations filled the air.

Pranav stole a few glances at his companion. The feeling of familiarity gnawed at him, but he couldn't quite place it.

"May I sit by the window?" she asked suddenly, breaking his thoughts.

"Of course." he switched seats without hesitation.

(Technically, she was asking—but since she was already sitting in his seat, it felt more like a soft takeover than a polite request!)

For a while, they sat in comfortable silence, the landscape outside changing from urban sprawl to open fields. Pranav finally found his voice. "Are you from Delhi?"

"No, Lucknow," she answered. "I had an interview yesterday at a Bank in Connaught Place. Now I'm heading home."

She paused before adding, "Father suggested I take the Lucknow Mail—said it would be the sensible thing to do. But I told him, why should I spend a whole night rattling in a train when I could sleep peacefully in a hotel and take the Shatabdi in the morning? He didn't argue after that."

Pranav nodded. "A wise decision."

They sipped their complimentary tea in silence. Pranav turned her name over in his mind, fitting it against the puzzle of his memory. And then, it clicked.

He cleared his throat. "I'm Pranav Sharma."

"Aparna Mishra," she said, as if testing the name in her own voice.

Pranav felt a fleeting urge to say, "Yes, I know," but, restrained by the polite conventions of the moment, he simply offered, "Nice to meet you, Ms. Aparna," all the while amused by the irony of his own formality.

The confirmation sent a ripple through him. A name from the past, now seated beside him, unaware.

He hesitated before speaking again. "Hey, I used to be called Manu. Do you—?"

Aparna frowned, looking at him properly for the first time. "Excuse me, but why are you staring at me?"

Pranav flushed. "I'm sorry. I didn't mean to make you uncomfortable. It's just... you look familiar."

She raised an eyebrow. "Oh? That's the best line you've got?"

"No, no! I mean it. You really do look familiar."

She crossed her arms, skeptical. "Alright, then. Prove it."

Pranav leaned back, smiling. "And if I do?"

"Convince me, and you might get my number. Maybe even a coffee."

"And if I fail?"

"No more talking until we reach Lucknow. Deal?"

Pranav grinned. "Deal."

There was something thrilling about this moment—a playful game, a test of memory and fate.

"I know what you're thinking," he said confidently. "But we do know each other."

"How?" Her gaze settling on Pranav's face with an intensity that carried both curiosity and quiet respect.

Aparna studied him, her fingers absently tracing the rim of her cup. A faint crease appeared between her brows, as if she too was trying to place him in some forgotten corner of her past.

Pranav, amused by her sudden scrutiny, ran his fingers over his cheeks, as if the answer might be hidden there. It had been two days since his last shave, and for a fleeting moment, he wondered if a rebellious stubble had emerged to betray him. But the smooth skin beneath his touch brought a sense of relief—at least, he thought, he appeared presentable for this unexpected examination.

"Shall I begin?" he asked, mischief dancing in his eyes.

She nodded, intrigued.

And so, as the train swayed gently along the tracks, Pranav prepared to bring the past rushing back, one memory at a time.

CHAPTER 2

Ding-dong...

The announcement crackled through the speakers—an invitation to pay attention—but the occupants of this particular compartment barely noticed. Announcements, after all, rarely told stories worth listening to.

"Ladies and Gentlemen," the voice floated through the compartment, calm and unhurried, as if the speaker had all the time in the world. "Allow me to tell you a story—not of where we are, but of a place you may one day find yourself longing to visit. A place called Lucknow—a city that wears history as one wears an old, beloved shawl, soft and familiar."

The train, steady and rhythmic—clickety-clack, clickety-clack—seemed to lean in, as if eager to hear the city's tales.

"Lucknow, they say, has watched empires rise and fall—from the Delhi Sultanate to the grandeur of the Mughals, from the elegance of the Nawabs of Awadh to the stern footfalls of the British. And yet, through it all, the city remained itself—gracious, patient, and distinctly charming."

"Now, if you ever stroll through its narrow lanes—and you should, though they may seem determined to let you lose your way—you'll find the air richly seasoned. Spices, yes, but also stories. Here, even a cup of chai comes with a conversation, and every passerby seems to know a tale worth telling."

"And speaking of tales—there is one you must remember. It is about Tundey ke Kabab, a name that carries both flavor and folklore. The story goes that Nawab Asaf-ud-Daula, a man of fine taste but failing teeth, yearned for a kebab so tender it would dissolve on the tongue. It was Haji Murad Ali—a man with only one arm but a heart full of culinary genius—who created a masterpiece. With a secret blend of spices known to him alone, he gave the Nawab his wish, and gave the world a legend."

"In Lucknow, you see, even food comes with a backstory—and backstories often last longer than the meal."

"But then, that is Lucknow for you: a city that never rushes, never boasts, but always lingers—on your tongue, in your heart, and most certainly, in your memory."

The train wheels hummed a metallic lullaby as Aparna rested her head against the window, watching the countryside blur like a half-remembered dream. Fields of green and lone palm trees blurred into a fleeting canvas, and the golden sunlight, fractured by the glass, painted fleeting patterns on her face. She let the crackle of the overhead announcement drift past her ears—mere noise, unworthy of disturbing her reverie.

Beside her, Pranav reclined with an air of quiet mischief, his eyes alight with something unsaid. His smile held a story, carefully stowed away for just the right moment. Aparna felt it, the delicious weight of a secret begging for release.

"So," she asked, her voice threading through the ambient hum, "when will you finally tell me?"

Pranav's smile deepened, as though savoring his advantage. "Patience," he replied, his tone rich with playful mystery. "Let's wait for breakfast. That's when the story will find its time."

The attendant's cart rattled into view, the man neat and efficient in his movements. Pranav, his voice carrying a flourish, placed his order. "Bread cutlet and Bournvita—ah, no, let's have tea instead." His manner lent gravity to this minor indulgence, as if each choice were part of the unfolding tale.

Aparna, her eyes dancing, countered, "The same for me—only, coffee." Her words landed lightly, a thread in their unspoken game.

When breakfast arrived, the warm clink of cups and the aroma of tea and coffee seemed to mark the prelude to something more.

Aparna, leaning forward with an expectant smile, pressed him, "Now that breakfast is over, let's hear it."

Between them was a warmth, shaped by ease and memory, though Aparna felt something more—a tug at the edge of recollection. Pranav's manner teased familiarity, like a long-forgotten melody played from another room. She searched the corners of her mind—a classroom, a voice from a season gone by—just out of reach.

Pranav's expression shifted, like a storyteller gathering the first threads of his tale. "This is a story of two children," he began, his voice settling into the steady rhythm of memory. "A boy and a girl, much like us. It was the summer of 1992, in the heart of Lucknow..."

The train pressed on, steel and earth in quiet harmony. And within its cradle, two stories began their slow unravelling—one spoken, one remembered, each promising to meet at the same destination.

CHAPTER 3

Year 1992:

Aliganj, a vibrant quarter of Lucknow, woke each morning like an old storyteller—hesitant at first, then easing into familiar, bustling tales. The city clung to its past with one hand while reaching toward the future with the other. The streets were timeless. At dawn, water sprinkled on dusty lanes released an earthy fragrance that mingled with the sweet aroma of chai. The milkman, balancing shiny containers on his bicycle, announced his arrival with a rhythmic clang, while a vegetable vendor stretched and yawned, preparing for another day of spirited bargaining.

As the sun warmed the rooftops, the locality stirred with its usual energy. Scooters sputtered awake with their signature cough, rickshaws groaned as they ferried passengers, and bicycles wove like determined dragonflies through the traffic. Street vendors displayed their wares with theatrical flair: heaps of golden mangoes, bundles of coriander still damp from the fields, and toys that clicked and whirred when cranked. The sounds of morning blended into a familiar symphony: the metallic whir of the knife-sharpener's wheel, the rhythmic beat of a cobbler's hammer, and the crackling melody of an old Kishore Kumar song spilling from a paan shop's dusty radio.

By mid-morning, the streets had transformed into a living maze of purpose and chatter. Schoolchildren, shirts stained with ink and adventure, raced along the footpaths, their laughter mingling with the sharp tring-tring of passing cycles. Office-goers, armed with steel tiffins and hurried expressions, navigated the chaos with practiced ease. From a shaded bench, an elderly man fiddled with his transistor radio, muttering about politics as crackling voices read out the morning headlines.

"Janab, the kebabs are fresh today," called out a vendor, his voice blending with the sizzle of the grill. In Lucknow, even greetings came with poetry.

The air swirled with the rich scent of coal-fired kebabs, the citrus tang of freshly cut coriander, and the comforting warmth of chai bubbling on stoves. Street vendors gestured with theatrical flair, inviting passersby to admire golden mangoes and glossy bangles. And always, beneath the bustle, the city's quiet rhythm endured—patient, poetic, and unmistakably Lucknow.

The city existed on its own terms. Autorickshaws, black with yellow roofs, whizzed past, their radios crackling with old Bollywood hits. Children skipped by, singing the latest Kumar Sanu tune as if it were a nursery rhyme. Here, time moved not by the ticking of clocks but by the rhythms of daily life. The presence of black rotary telephones and Bush radios crackling with cricket commentary hinted at the era's simplicity.

Among these lanes, hidden like a secret, was Mehndi Tola—a pocket of quiet amid the city's commotion. It was a place of narrow lanes, shaded courtyards, and walls that bore the faded strokes of past festivals. In one of the houses, modest yet proud, lived a woman with her younger son. Her husband had passed on years ago, leaving behind a sepia-toned photograph and a legacy of stories. Her daughter lived in a government colony nearby, and her eldest son worked in Delhi. Yet the house never truly felt empty— especially during the summers.

That was when her eldest grandson, Pranav, seven years old and fresh from Delhi for his summer vacation, arrived, bringing with him the infectious energy of a squirrel in a fruit-laden tree. His arrival was always announced by the squeal of the iron gate and the delighted chatter of neighborhood children. The moment he stepped in, the scent of incense and the murmur of the morning prayer welcomed him, with the Gayatri Mantra floating softly in the air. The small temple in the corner stood like a vigilant guardian, and beside it, the guava tree leaned toward the veranda, as if curious to catch the stories unfolding below.

The house, with its sunlit courtyard and creaky wooden staircase, seemed to breathe along with its inhabitants. Its kitchen smelled of ghee, cardamom, and the occasional whiff of pickles fermenting on the window ledge. On the terrace, time stood still, interrupted only by cricket matches that ended with arguments about whether the ball was out or not.

The upper rooms were rented to a family, and among them was girl, seven years old, a sharp-eyed girl with a knack for challenging every statement. Her elder brother, nine years old, a quiet observer of their antics, often served as the umpire in their terrace matches. Summers were incomplete without her—they argued, laughed, and conspired with the intensity only childhood can muster.

Mornings began with a tilak on Pranav's forehead, a ritual as consistent as the jalebis and khasta kachoris that followed. Afternoons were spent in the old library, fingers tracing the cracked leather of forgotten books. Evenings were for cricket, carrom, and covert explorations of the attic, where mysteries surely hid in the shadows.

But time, indifferent to their escapades, moved on. The endless summers gave way to school schedules. By the late nineties, Pranav's visits grew sporadic. When he finally returned, the upstairs rooms were empty; the girl and her family had moved, leaving only echoes behind. Life moved on.

Until, twelve years later, a train journey turned the clock backward. Beside him sat a girl with familiar eyes.

August, 2009: Back to train

He spoke of summer afternoons and cricket match on sun-warmed terraces, of stolen mangoes and sugarcane juice breaks. As he spoke, her brow furrowed, and her grip on the cup tightened.

She thought, "The house you describe… it sounds just like the one I lived in till 1997."

Outside, the fields blurred past like fleeting memories on a forgotten film reel. Inside, the air thickened with something unspoken.

Pranav smiled and kept talking. As he described the garden with the guava tree that leaned conspiratorially toward the veranda, the crack of the cricket bat, and the shared victories over carrom matches, she froze.

Her heart raced. Her breath caught.

"No…" she whispered, eyes wide. "How do you know all this?"

Pranav leaned back, a familiar grin spreading across his face. "Because," he said, extending his phone toward her, "you owe me a feast. And I need your number to remind you."

Aparna gasped. Her heart fluttered like a sparrow startled into flight. Memories surged—of sunlit afternoons, of mango pulp smeared across faces, of whispered secrets beneath the stairs.

"Manu!" she shrieked, the name bursting from her like a child's squeal at a magic trick.

The compartment fell silent. Passengers looked up from newspapers and novels. Aparna didn't notice. Her laughter spilled out—wild, unfiltered, and brimming with disbelief.

The story had worked a small miracle. Aparna had finally recognized her childhood friend, Pranav.

But recognition, like most things in life, has its consequences.

The way she had shouted "Manu!" had caught not only Pranav's attention but also that of the entire compartment. Conversations paused, newspapers were lowered, and heads turned as if someone had declared an emergency. The passengers eyed Pranav with suspicion.

A young man across the aisle leaned forward, his voice firm. "Is everything all right, madam?"

"Is he bothering you?" asked another, narrowing his eyes at Pranav.

A college boy, feeling brave in front of his audience, stood up with exaggerated confidence. 'Madam, you can sit here if you like. We'll take care of him."

"No violence," an elderly man advised. "Call the railway police. They will handle the matter."

Aparna, still breathless with laughter, raised her hands. "No, no! Everything is fine. He's my childhood friend, and we're meeting after twelve years. I got a bit carried away. I'm so sorry for disturbing you."

The crowd relaxed, but not before casting Pranav a few lingering, distrustful glances. For a moment, she could hardly believe it herself. Manu—here, after all these years.

Aparna shook her head with a laugh. "Manu... who would have thought?"

"Thanks!" Pranav said, shaking his head. "You almost got me arrested today."

"I'm sorry, Manu. I just forgot where I was," Aparna said, cheeks flushed with embarrassment.

Pranav gave a weary sigh and leaned back. His gaze shifted to the window, where fields stretched out endlessly. He ran a hand through his hair and muttered to himself: "If I had known I was meeting my childhood friend today, I would've dressed better."

He looked down at his faded blue jeans and the plain white T-shirt, which seemed, at that moment, thoroughly unimpressive.

"Damn," he thought, "I wish I could have hidden somewhere. Or at least changed my seat."

The years melted away like mist in the morning sun. The train rattled on, oblivious to the reunion it carried—and the journey it had just set in motion.

CHAPTER 4

The train moved through the countryside with a sense of quiet amusement, its wheels tapping out a tune like a drummer testing his sticks before a grand performance. In the chair car coach, Aparna and Pranav sat side by side, their faces lit with the glow of rediscovered friendship. The train, if it had a voice, might have chuckled at their excitement—it had carried many passengers before, but few who spoke with the unguarded delight of two children who had found a long-lost treasure.

Suddenly, the speakers crackled to life with the familiar distortion of a train announcement: "Attention passengers, we will shortly arrive at Kanpur Central. Please check your belongings."

The voice hovered above them like a school principal announcing exam dates—dull, uninvited, and easily ignored. Outside the window, Kanpur stretched and stirred, ready for another busy day. Leather tanneries rumbled awake, tea vendors lined the platform, their kettles releasing twisting ribbons of steam into the crisp morning air. The train slowed, its brakes sighing in disappointment. In the distance, the Ganga glimmered in the afternoon sun—calm, timeless, and unaware of the passing train. Inside the coach, the hum of the air-conditioning softened the sounds of the bustling station beyond.

But Pranav and Aparna heard none of it. Their laughter floated above the hum of the train, as if time itself had paused to listen to the stories of two childhood friends who had found each other again.

The train left Kanpur with a satisfied sigh, gathering speed as passengers scrambled to find their seats. Bags thudded into overhead racks, hawkers called out for chai and samosas, and a child wailed somewhere in the distance. Through it all, Aparna and Pranav sat undisturbed, lost in their own world. The train, satisfied with the sights of the passing countryside, seemed to shift its attention inward, as though settling down to listen to the conversation unfolding between its two curious passengers.

"So, Manu," Aparna said, turning toward him with a curious smile. "What are you doing these days? How is everyone back home?"

Pranav shifted in his seat and stretched his legs as far as the cramped space allowed. The dark green seats, with their maze of faded patterns, creaked softly as he leaned back. He ran a hand along the armrest, where the paint on the edges had worn away from years of restless elbows. "Well, I enrolled myself in the Chartered Accountancy course."

"CA?" Aparna's eyebrows arched in surprise. "That sounds complicated."

"It is," Pranav said with a sigh. "Right now, I'm preparing for my Professional Competency Exam. It's the second level of the CA course, after the Common Proficiency Test." He traced a finger across the plastic tray table, leaving a faint line on the dusty surface. "I appeared for the June 2009 exam but... missed the passing mark by two marks. Two marks. That was all it took to turn months of hard work into a red 'Fail' on the screen. I sat there, numb, wondering how something as small as a single digit could carry so much weight."

"Two marks?" Aparna's eyes widened. "Two measly marks?"

"Exactly!" Pranav said, sitting up. "Two marks! And I studied so hard that even the tax laws started appearing on the bathroom tiles. When the results were announced, I checked them online on the ICAI website. I stared at the screen for a full minute, hoping my eyes had made a mistake. But the numbers didn't change. And then, somewhere from within me, a voice whispered, 'Better luck next time.' "

Aparna laughed softly. "That must have stung."

"It did," Pranav said, adjusting his glasses. "But that's not all. Along with the exams, there's the articleship—a mandatory training period."

"Articleship?"

"Yes," Pranav explained, resting his arm on the seat's foldable tray. "It's three years and six months of articleship, which I'm doing under a Chartered Accountancy firm in Lajpat Nagar, New Delhi.

"And how's that going?"

Pranav rubbed his forehead. "Let's just say they believe that calculators are infallible. I have to recheck every figure twice—once for accuracy, and once for their satisfaction."

Aparna chuckled. "Sounds like you're earning that CA degree the hard way."

"The very hard way," Pranav said with a grin. "But I suppose I've always liked numbers. They behave better than people. You add, subtract, multiply, and divide—and they do exactly what you ask."

The train gave a sudden jolt, and the window glass vibrated with a low hum, like a murmuring old man clearing his throat. The countryside rolled by without a care, while inside, two friends sat talking—oblivious to the journey that was taking them closer to an old city and a thousand half-forgotten memories.

"Enough about me," Pranav said, leaning forward with interest. "What about you, Aparna? What are you doing these days?"

Aparna smiled and adjusted her spectacles with one hand, while the other smoothed the loose end of her blue kurti. The train rattled on, and a beam of sunlight squeezed through the narrow window, falling across her face. It lit up her cheeks and glinted off her glasses, making her squint slightly as she spoke. The sunlight, like a curious visitor, lingered there as if eager to listen in. The gold border of her earrings caught the light, casting tiny patterns on her neck with each sway of the train.

"Well, after school, I did my B.Sc. from Lucknow University. I actually wanted to do B.Tech, but..." She trailed off and tapped her fingers on the armrest. The soft thud of her nails against the plastic merged with the steady clatter of the wheels beneath them. "Papa said that since my brother was already doing B.Tech, the fees would be too much for the family. So, I took up B.Sc. instead."

"That must have been hard," Pranav said softly.

"It was," Aparna admitted. "I sulked for days, pacing across the terrace like a restless cat. But Papa just smiled and said, 'You'll understand someday.' I never understood what he meant until much later. Anyway, after completing my B.Sc., I did my MBA, and now I'm preparing for bank competitive exams."

Pranav gave a low whistle. "Bank exams? Impressive."

"Yes," Aparna said, adjusting her spectacles again as the sunlight shifted. "I think my father somehow knew we'd meet on this train. Maybe that's why he asked me not to join B.Tech."

They both laughed, the sound rising above the low murmur of the compartment and mingling with the rhythmic clatter of the wheels. Outside, the fields stretched endlessly, indifferent to the conversation of two childhood friends who had found each other after a dozen years.

The train, which had been their silent companion all along, stirred with a familiar mix of emotions. It had seen countless passengers board, chat, and part ways, but these two—these childhood friends—were different. Their laughter carried the weight of shared secrets; their silences were thick with unspoken memories. The train had welcomed them like an old host receiving long-lost guests, and now, as the journey neared its end, it wasn't quite sure how to feel.

The wheels beneath groaned softly, slowing as if to delay the inevitable. It had tried its best—slipping a beam of sunlight through the tinted glass onto the girl's face, letting the window panels vibrate just enough to make the boy glance at her with recognition. It had even softened its familiar clatter, hoping not to intrude on the stories that flowed like a gentle stream. And yet, time marched on, indifferent to the train's desires.

The countryside beyond the sealed windows blurred into the outskirts of Lucknow. Buildings replaced open fields; their shapes distorted through the slightly frosted glass. The cabin remained cocooned in cool, filtered air, carrying the faint metallic scent of recycled ventilation. The train sighed, releasing a whisper of air through the vents. Lucknow—the city where their journey would end, and their story might begin.

The speakers crackled overhead, preparing to deliver their routine message. But even the speaker, it seemed, wasn't ready to break the spell. The sound wavered, as though unsure of itself—crackling, sputtering, and then falling into silence. The train's wheels clinked below, offering the speaker some encouragement. Finally, with what felt like a heavy heart, the announcement returned:

"Yeh... yeh gaadi... kuch hi samay mein Lucknow Jn... par pahunchegi... Kripya apne... saamaan ki dekhbhal karein... Muskuraiye, aap Lucknow pahunchnay waale hain."

The words hung in the air for a moment, like an uninvited guest. Muskuraiye—smile. The irony wasn't lost on the train. It was asking its passengers to smile when it, itself, felt a lump of sorrow in its metallic heart. Lucknow was known as the city of etiquette, of grace, of welcoming smiles. But the train, despite its years of travel, had never learned to hide its emotions.

The compartment stirred to life. Bags were tugged from overhead racks. Conversations turned to hotel bookings and family visits. Phones buzzed with unread messages. The faint clink of plastic trays being folded echoed softly across the aisle. The train felt the shift—like a storyteller whose tale had been interrupted before the final chapter.

But the two friends remained untouched by the commotion. Their conversation, woven with childhood mischief and shared ambitions, floated above the hum of the air conditioning. The train slowed further, wheels clicking across a bridge like a drumroll at the end of a performance. It leaned ever so slightly to the right, as if peeking into the station to glimpse what lay ahead.

Lucknow Junction came into view: the red-brick platform bathed in afternoon light, porters in crisp uniforms navigating luggage with practiced ease, vendors adjusting their carts laden with paper cups of chai and plates of hot pakoras. The train sighed again—a long, weary sigh of farewell. It was happy, of course. Happy that it had been the stage for a reunion twelve years in the making. But there was sadness, too. Like a friendly neighbor watching children grow up and move away, the train knew its part was over.

"Lucknow," Pranav said softly, glancing out through the tinted window.

"Yes," Aparna replied, adjusting her spectacles. "But somehow, it feels like the journey's just begun."

The train smiled—if a train could smile. It glided into the station, brakes hissing in resignation. It had brought them together, yes. But what came next? Would they wander the streets of Lucknow like they had the fields of childhood? Would they part ways again, carried away by life's obligations?

The train did not know. All it knew was that its role was done. It came to a gentle halt, the last click of the wheels sounding like the full stop at the end of a sentence.

And as passengers bustled past, the train stood still, listening one last time for the laughter that had turned a routine journey into something unforgettable.

CHAPTER 5

Lucknow station stood like a grand sentinel from a forgotten era, dressed in its signature red and white. The domes, pristine and rounded like chess pawns, seemed to nod approvingly beneath the afternoon sun. The symmetrical arches stretched along the platform, stately and unyielding, their brickwork warmed by decades of arrivals and farewells. Palm trees lined the approach, their fronds drooping in the heat, while shadows lay curled at their roots like tired pets.

The station hadn't witnessed the reunion; it had only seen two passengers stepping off the train together. But the train, unwilling to let the moment go, had whispered it to the station in its final breath. And so, the platform welcomed them with quiet curiosity, as though it knew that these two were not just any travelers, but threads of a story that had been rejoined after years of separation.

The air shimmered with heat, bending the outlines of the station nameboard like a mirage. Porters moved sluggishly, their shirts sticking to their backs as they hauled suitcases and bundles wrapped in old bedsheets. A chai vendor stood beside his cart, wiping his forehead with a crumpled towel before calling out, "Chai, garam chai!"—less an invitation, more a declaration of duty. A stray dog dozed beneath a bench; its ears twitching whenever a suitcase thudded to the ground.

Behind them, the train lingered for a moment longer, its engine releasing a deep, metallic sigh—a whisper of farewell to the two friends it had carried together after so many years. Then, with a shudder of resignation, it turned away and fell silent, watching them being greeted by the city that had just opened its arms.

The station watched as they made their way toward the exit. Aparna spoke with the ease of someone meeting an old friend after years apart—her words tumbling out in lively streams. The air around them seemed to pause, curious to catch the thread of her excitement. Sunlight streamed through the arches, dancing on the platform floor as if eager to join the conversation.

Pranav walked beside her, his bag slung over one shoulder, offering the occasional nod or smile. A pigeon, startled by her animated voice, fluttered away from the ticket counter, its wings flapping like an indignant protest.

They stepped out of the station, leaving the shade of the arched veranda behind. The afternoon heat greeted them with a shimmering wave, and the pavement radiated warmth through their soles. The prepaid auto stand stood a few yards ahead, marked by a faded yellow board. A small queue stretched toward the booth, where a clerk with a red pen behind his ear tapped the counter with impatient fingers.

"Shall we?" Pranav asked, gesturing toward the stand.

Aparna didn't respond. She was still talking, her eyes bright, her voice animated. The sun watched, amused, as the two friends moved toward the queue—one speaking without pause, the other smiling without complaint.

The prepaid auto stand hummed with the usual chaos of midday travel. The clerk behind the counter tapped his pen on the wooden surface with the resigned patience of a man who had long accepted his fate. Passengers shuffled forward in a slow-moving queue, auto drivers leaned lazily against their vehicles, and a stray dog napped under the shade of a parked scooter, oblivious to the heat and the world's concerns.

Aparna stood beside Pranav, speaking with the same cheerful ease that had accompanied her through the train journey. "We shifted to Jankipuram in 1997," she said, adjusting her spectacles. "But Lucknow never really felt new to me. How could it? We practically lived in your Dadi's house back then."

Pranav smiled. "Yeah. I remember those afternoons at the library. We mostly pretended to read while trying to guess which shelf the ghost lived in."

"Exactly!" Aparna laughed. "And the evenings on the terrace... cricket, carrom, and that broken swing where we'd sit, plotting grand plans to explore the attic."

Pranav gave a soft chuckle. The memories came easily—summer afternoons when the scent of ripe mangoes hung in the air, and the thrill of treasure hunts that ended with sunburned cheeks and scraped knees.

"You know," Aparna said, nudging him lightly with her elbow, "you should call me sometime. We can catch up properly. Talk about something other than... trains."

Pranav opened his mouth to respond but stopped himself, waiting. He had noticed her pattern—she rarely paused long enough for anyone else to contribute. Sure enough, Aparna was already mid-sentence again, recounting an amusing incident from her last trip to Delhi.

The queue inched forward. A rickety auto rattled past, its driver honking with the dedication of someone determined to turn noise into art.

Finally, Aparna paused to take a breath.

"I won't call you," Pranav said, his voice calm.

Aparna froze mid-spectacle-adjustment. "What?"

"I said I won't call you." He shrugged.

Her eyes widened. "Why not? Am I that bad? Do I talk too much? Or—wait—you think I won't answer? I know I forget to return calls sometimes, but that's no reason to write me off entirely!"

Pranav bit his lip to hide a grin. "No, it's not that."

"Then what?" she demanded, hands on her waist.

"Well... for me to call, you'd have to give me your number first."

Aparna's expression shifted from indignation to surprise. Her mouth formed a silent "Oh!" as realization dawned.

"I forgot to give it to you on the train!" she exclaimed, slapping her forehead. "That's your fault, by the way."

Pranav raised an eyebrow. "My fault?"

"Yes!" she said, wagging a finger at him. "I protected you from those passengers after I yelled 'Manu.' Remember? Everyone was staring at you like you were stalking me, and I had to explain you were my childhood friend. In all that excitement, I forgot!"

Pranav laughed. "Ah, yes. My rescuer. I'd have been hauled off to the railway police if not for you."

"Exactly!" Aparna said triumphantly, holding out her phone. "Now, save my number. And don't make me protect you again."

Pranav took out his phone, his thumb hovering over the keypad as she dictated the digits.

"Next!" barked the clerk from the counter.

They stepped forward to the counter. Aparna leaned over slightly. "One auto for Jankipuram, one for Keshav Puram," she said, pulling out two slightly crumpled ₹100 notes and handing them to the clerk.

Pranav's eyes widened. "How did you know about Keshav Puram?"

Aparna smiled. "Oh, I've been to your bua's house many times. Her chole bhature and khasta kachori are famous, remember?"

Pranav rubbed his chin thoughtfully. "Right. I'd forgotten about that."

As the clerk handed her the receipts, Pranav pulled out his wallet. "Here... at least let me pay for mine."

Aparna turned toward him with narrowed eyes. "Excuse me?"

Pranav hesitated. "I mean... you booked both autos, so—"

Aparna's jaw tightened. Her lips pressed into a thin line, and her eyes locked onto his with the intensity of a school teacher catching a student mid-prank.

Pranav swallowed. "Okay... okay..."

"Put that wallet back," she said, voice low but firm.

"Yes, ma'am," Pranav mumbled, stuffing the wallet into his pocket with exaggerated obedience. Then he pressed his palms together in mock surrender and added, "Sorry, ma'am."

Aparna's glare softened into a grin. "That's better. Next time, let me pay without drama."

They walked toward the waiting autos. Pranav placed his bag on the seat, hesitated for a moment, and turned back.

"Well... goodbye, Aparna," he said, his voice lighter than he felt.

"Not goodbye," Aparna corrected, brushing a stray strand of hair from her forehead. "Just... see you later."

"Right. See you later," Pranav echoed, gripping the auto's side handle.

The engine sputtered to life, and the auto jerked forward. Through the thinning crowd, Aparna stood waving—a familiar silhouette against the bustling backdrop of Lucknow Junction.

Pranav settled into his seat as the auto turned onto the main road. His phone vibrated softly in his pocket. He pulled it out, frowning. No new message, no missed call. Just the home screen, glowing faintly in the afternoon light.

Low battery.

It had been a silent companion through the journey—listening, watching, but never once interrupting. Not a single call. Not a single distraction. It had heard the stories, the laughter, the hesitant exchanges that turned strangers into friends.

And it had heard the promise.

A coffee treat, declared with playful certainty. A promise half fulfilled and half pending.

It had witnessed the moment when Aparna laid down the condition: Convince me, and you might get my number. Maybe even a coffee.

The number had been won. The call had been secured. But the coffee? Still a mystery.

And so, the phone waited.

For a call that might come tomorrow. Or next week. Or never.

Pranav chuckled, shook his head, and slipped the phone back into his pocket.

The auto turned onto the main road, the city stretching out before him. But in the confines of his pocket, the phone remained hopeful.

It had heard the promise. It would wait.

CHAPTER 6

The auto jolted forward with a metallic cough, and the mobile phone nestled in Pranav's pocket stirred. It had been a morning of surprises, and the phone, like an eager storyteller, tried to share the tale with the auto.

"He met his childhood friend today," the phone whispered. "Aparna Mishra. After twelve years. She called him 'Manu'—in front of everyone."

The auto rumbled dismissively, more interested in the tune on the crackling radio—Main Nikla Gaddi Leke. The old song floated through the air, and the auto followed its rhythm, oblivious to the phone's excitement.

Pranav tapped the phone's keypad absently—a habit from hours of texting and playing Snake during study breaks. The soft tap-tap-tap seemed in sync with his thoughts.

"He's remembering her," the phone murmured, recognizing the pattern. "That train ride. The laughter. The coffee promise."

Outside, Lucknow bustled—rickshaw bells jingled, vendors shouted, and the aroma of khasta kachoris drifted in. The auto veered left into a quieter lane shaded by neem trees. The familiar smell of chole bhature grew stronger.

"Bhaiya, yahin rok do," Pranav said.

The auto braked with a sigh. Pranav stepped out, slinging his bag over his shoulder. The gate creaked open, releasing the unmistakable scent of Bua's kitchen.

The auto rattled away, unbothered by the phone's story. The mobile sighed internally—another listener lost to indifference.

The phone, however, hummed softly in its pocket. As the aroma of chole bhature wafted through the air, it recognized the dish from Pranav's past searches. "His favorite," the phone mused, "and hers too."

Pranav entered the familiar courtyard. Gravel crunched beneath his feet. Bua appeared in a maroon cotton saree, wiping her hands on her pallu.

"Arre, Manu beta! I was waiting for you!"

"Bua!" Pranav greeted with a smile.

She fussed over him, ruffled his hair, and ushered him inside. "Go freshen up. Your chole bhature are waiting."

"Just five minutes," Pranav said, stretching.

The phone jostled in his pocket as he walked toward the bathroom down the hall. It heard the splash of water, the clink of the steel mug against the bucket. With each passing second, its battery bar dimmed.

"He hasn't charged me yet," the phone murmured. "How am I supposed to hear his thoughts if I go silent?"

Pranav returned, hair damp, face refreshed. The dining table awaited him with a gleaming steel plate, crowned by golden-brown bhature and a bowl of chole. He tore into the bhatura, releasing a crackling sound as steam escaped. The phone heard his satisfied sigh.

"He remembers to eat," the phone grumbled. "But not to charge me. Priorities!"

After the meal, exhaustion weighed on him. The 3:30 a.m. start and the train journey had caught up. He dropped onto the bed, his limbs surrendering to the soft mattress.

"Now," the phone whispered, "now would be the perfect time. Just plug me in."

Pranav's breathing slowed. The fan above hummed, matching the phone's soft pulses of energy.

Low Battery – 2%.

"Just one charge," the phone pleaded silently. "One cable, one socket, one touch."

Pranav snored softly.

1%...

"That's it? After everything I did today? The train, the coffee promise... and now? Ignored like a missed call."

The phone vibrated weakly; its final plea unheard.

Screen off. Battery drained. Silence.

Afternoon slipped away quietly, unnoticed—just like the phone's final breath.

Pranav stirred, shifting his head on the pillow. His hand reached instinctively for his phone. The device lay lifeless beside him. He pressed the power button. Nothing happened.

He scanned the wall socket. The charger lay coiled on the bedside table like a waiting snake. Pranav plugged it in. Within seconds, the screen flickered to life.

Charging... 2%.

"Finally!" the phone exhaled in relief.

The fan above hummed gently, its blades slicing the air.

"If only the fan knew what I know," the phone mused. "But how could it? It just swirls around all day without leaving the room."

Before the phone could dwell on this, the door creaked open.

"Manu! Get up! Tea's ready," Bua called.

Pranav yawned and left the room. The phone hummed contentedly as the battery indicator inched upward.

The fan continued its lazy rotations.

"So," the fan whispered, tilting toward the bedside table. "What's this about Aparna? I heard something earlier."

The phone gave a soft vibration. "He met her on the train. Childhood friends. Recognized her right away. Aparna didn't remember at first. He told her stories from their summers together. And then she shouted 'Manu!' right there in the train."

"Manu?" The fan whirred with curiosity. "That must've caused a stir."

"Oh, it did!" the phone continued. "The passengers thought he was stalking her! Aparna had to explain it to everyone."

"Typical train crowd," the fan muttered. "And then what?"

"She promised him a coffee treat if he could prove their connection. He did. But she forgot to give him her number until the auto stand."

"Ah," the fan sighed. "And now?"

"Bua just called Aparna's mother. They're meeting tomorrow at six," the phone buzzed proudly.

The fan slowed slightly. "Tomorrow? That soon?"

"Yes," the phone replied. "The story continues."

Beneath them, the bed creaked softly, unnoticed at first. The fan turned, puzzled.

"Wait," it whispered. "Did you hear that?"

"What?" the phone asked.

The bed gave a low groan. "Tomorrow? They're meeting tomorrow?"

"Yes," the phone said, surprised.

"Oh," the bed murmured. "That means... we'll get to hear more of the story?"

"Of course," the phone assured it. "And I promise to tell you everything."

"Good," said the bed, giving a pleased creak. "I haven't been this excited since Manu was a boy."

The fan adjusted its speed. "Phone, promise me something."

"What?"

"Tomorrow, when they return, tell us everything. Every word. Every moment."

The phone's screen blinked softly. "I promise."

The fan sighed and resumed its rhythmic hum. The bed creaked once more, then stilled.

Just then, the aroma of dal and rice wafted in from the kitchen.

"Ah, dinner time," the bed said with an anticipatory groan.

Pranav returned to the dining area, where Bua served steaming dal-chawal with ghee. Phuphaji set down a tub of butterscotch ice cream.

After the meal, no one said much; the satisfaction of a good dinner made words unnecessary.

Pranav stretched out on the bed. The bed responded by molding slightly, cradling him like royalty.

"The king returns," the bed whispered.

"Indeed," the fan added, sending a cool breeze.

Pranav's eyes drooped. "Phone," the fan whispered. "Don't forget. Tomorrow."

"I won't," the phone promised.

The bed hummed. "Ah, young love."

The fan chuckled and turned toward morning.

The next evening arrived with a sun that seemed too curious to hide behind clouds. It stretched its golden arms across the narrow lanes of Keshav Puram, watching with mild amusement as Bua and Pranav stepped out of the gate.

The mobile phone, snug in Pranav's pocket, hummed with excitement. It remembered the fan's request, the bed's anticipation, and the promise it had made: to report every word, every moment.

The scooty ride to Aparna's house began with the usual jolt. The phone braced itself as Pranav tapped absentmindedly at its keypad. "He's nervous," the phone noted. "Meeting an old friend twice in two days? Unusual. Meeting her at her home? Even more so."

Beside him, Bua adjusted her dupatta and launched into a steady stream of conversation about the changing seasons, the rising price of mustard oil, and how Monu's teachers gave contradictory advice about board exam preparation. Pranav nodded politely, though his eyes stayed fixed on the passing streets.

The phone, meanwhile, tried to share these insights with the scooty. "We're going to Aparna's house," it whispered through the faint hum of the engine.

The scooty responded by increasing its speed slightly, as if eager to deliver its passengers and resume its mechanical slumber.

The phone recognized Pranav's tightening grip on the handlebar and sensed his silent excitement.

"We're close," the phone whispered.

They stopped outside a modest, cream-colored house with a neatly swept entrance.

"Here we are," Bua announced, stepping off. "Come on, Manu."

The phone heard the faint click of the gate opening and the crunch of gravel beneath Pranav's shoes.

The door swung open with the same energy as its occupant.

"Auntie!" Aparna exclaimed, eyes lighting up. "Manu!" Her voice carried the same breathless enthusiasm as the day before.

The phone noted how Pranav's shoulders relaxed. "That name," it thought. "Still magical. Still effective."

They entered the house, and from that moment, Aparna's words filled every corner. She spoke about her brother's unpredictable scooter, the neighbor's parrot that imitated phone ringtones, and the morning's struggle with a stubborn ceiling fan. She pointed at family photos on the wall, described each relative's quirks, and narrated the history of the guava tree outside.

The mobile phone recorded these bursts of conversation with patient fascination. Pranav, for his part, responded with occasional nods and chuckles.

Finally, over cups of elaichi tea, the conversation shifted.

Pranav leaned back with a teasing smile. "To bataiye, Ms. Aparna, is shahar-e-nawabi mein humein kahaan le jaayengi aap?" His voice carried a playful poetic tone.

Aparna adjusted her spectacles and smiled. "Arre, janaab," she responded with mock seriousness, "agar hum par yeh zimmedaari aayi, to hum aapko le jaayenge Lucknow ke dil mein... Ameenabad ki galiyon mein, jahan zubaan par swad rehta hai aur dilon mein Lucknowi tehzeeb."

"Wah!" Pranav clapped lightly. "Aur phir?"

"Phir," Aparna continued, "phir aapko dikhayenge Bada Imambada ka wo bhool-bhulaiya jismein rahein gayi hain kahaniyaan aur rishtey, jaise humare bachpan ki yaadein."

"Wah, wah!" Pranav said, laughing. "Ab main intezaar kaise karoon?"

"Intezaar mein bhi ek maza hai, janaab," Aparna said, raising an eyebrow. "Kal milenge Ameenabad ki galiyon mein."

The visit ended with Aparna walking them to the gate. She waved until the scooty disappeared from view.

Back at Bua's house, the phone lay proudly on the bedside table, fully charged and ready to report.

"Well?" the fan whispered, tilting slightly to look down.

"Ah, the chatter!" the phone began. "Non-stop. Breathless. Enthusiastic. Aparna didn't give poor Pranav a moment's silence."

The bed creaked softly. "And the plan?"

"Ameenabad tomorrow. Then Bada Imambada."

The fan whirred thoughtfully. "Food and history. Good combination."

The bed sighed contentedly. "A love story with proper planning," it said.

The phone's screen dimmed slightly as if smiling.

Outside, the moon peeked through the window, casting a silvery glow across the room.

"We've done our job," the fan whispered.

"For now," said the phone.

"Now what?" asked the bed.

"Now," the phone murmured, "we wait. We wait for the new love to blossom in the streets of Lucknow."

CHAPTER 7

The morning knew.

It had been a silent observer, standing in the shadows of the past few days, watching, listening, waiting. It had seen the clamor of the railway station, where old names had surfaced from a reservation chart like forgotten verses of a song. It had witnessed the auto stand, where voices had risen in playful banter, rickshaws had clattered away, and a journey had begun—not just across the city, but into the folds of something long-lost. It had stood by the door of a quiet house, where laughter had touched the walls like hesitant raindrops before settling into a steady downpour of familiarity.

The morning stretched its golden limbs across rooftops, nudging the city awake. It leaned against tea stalls where kettles began their daily symphony, brushed past sleepy courtyards where newspapers rustled in the breeze, and peered into lanes where the first cycle-rickshaw of the day rattled through. It slipped into a roadside paan shop, where a coal sigdi glowed red under the weight of roasting betel nuts, and lingered near a temple entrance, where pigeons shuffled on the warm stone steps.

It had heard whispers of promises, spoken casually the day before—of places to be visited, of streets to be walked, of stories yet to be written.

And so, it waited. For, footsteps to arrive. For voices to fill the silence. For another day to unfold.

The morning had settled into the comfort of the day, the heat beginning to creep in as the sun climbed higher. The streets, still not fully awake, seemed to stretch lazily under the gentle hum of the monsoon air.

Then, breaking the silence of the day, came the familiar hum of a scooty engine.

Aparna arrived, her two-wheeler rattling over the uneven road with a determined buzz. The air carried the smell of warm earth and frying samosas from the nearest corner shop. She pulled up effortlessly, tapping the side of her scooty, almost as if acknowledging the small triumph of the ride.

Without missing a beat, she turned to Pranav, her voice light and teasing: "Aapka driver hazir hai, janaab! Bas baithiye, hum aapko Ameenabad dikhayenge."

Pranav, settling behind her, adjusted his position and replied softly, almost to himself, in a poetic Urdu tone:

"Jahan bhi aap chalen, har kadam mein ek nayi baat hai,

Aapke saath safar, har raaste ki baat hai."

Her outfit was simple—just a plain cotton top that clung loosely to her frame and a pair of well-worn jeans, perfectly suited for the hot and humid day. The clothes seemed effortless, the kind that belonged to someone who knew the city well, who had walked its streets far too many times to be concerned with anything more than comfort.

Pranav, seated behind her, was dressed in a light cotton shirt and dark jeans, both practical for the weather, though his shirt was slightly tucked at the hem, giving him a more polished look than the streets around him demanded. His shirt sleeves were rolled up just enough to keep him cool but not quite enough to make him seem completely relaxed. The outfit wasn't flashy, but it suited him in a way that fit the quiet, introspective nature he carried with him.

He adjusted himself behind her, and with a slight wobble, they were off. The scooty zipped through the streets, and as they rode, the city slowly came to life.

A cycle-rickshaw trundled along, its driver yawning lazily as he pedaled through the heat. A chaiwala at a roadside stall expertly poured tea from a brass kettle, steam rising in the warm air. Nearby, a shopkeeper dusted off a display of colorful bangles, their bright hues gleaming under the sun.

At a corner, a young boy was slicing fresh guavas, rubbing them with salt and chili, his stall a small oasis in the midday heat.

The scooty sped past an old bookshop with half-open shutters, where a man sat on a stool, reading a thick Urdu novel, oblivious to the world. A tailor worked in his cramped space, adjusting a Lucknowi kurti, its delicate stitching almost as old as the city itself.

As they neared their destination, the roads narrowed, the houses crowded closer together, and the bustling sounds of the market began to hum in the distance. Ameenabad was coming into view.

Aparna, with a smile, turned to Pranav and said, "Chaliye janaab, Ameenabad ke dil mein hum aapka swagat kar rahe hain!"

Ameenabad's streets seemed to draw them in, as if they, too, had been waiting.

The sun blazed overhead, casting a golden light on Ameenabad, its midday heat pressing down on the narrow streets. The city, slow to react to the bustling world beyond its confines, seemed to pause for a moment, as if waiting for the afternoon heat to pass before life resumed its usual pace. For Pranav and Aparna, this was their first time walking these streets together and the place felt like a mystery waiting to be discovered, a chapter of their shared past that had never been written—until now.

Their steps echoed in the quiet warmth as they made their way through the narrow lanes, their familiar silence punctuated by small remarks—a quiet reminder of how things had once been. It was as though they had stepped back in time, yet with the awareness of years gone by, and the lives they had led since then.

They had arrived at a small tea stall nestled between two shops, the familiar faces of locals catching glimpses of their presence. The chaiwala, an old man with a wrinkled face and worn-out sandals, served them tea with practiced ease, his movements steady, as though he had been making tea for the city's heart for years. The steam rose from the glass, filling the air with the smell of ginger and spices, a scent that felt like home. In this moment, the sense of their childhood seemed to return, whispering in the quiet hum of the city.

Aparna sipped her tea, glancing around with a quiet smile. The streets felt oddly familiar to her. She had walked these very roads before, with her friends during college days, and maybe with her parents before that, on weekends spent wandering through the heart of Ameenabad. The fragrant smells of spices, the colorful stalls lining the streets, and the familiar hum of chatter had been a part of her memories for years. But this time, it felt different—this time, she wasn't just passing through—she was sharing it with someone from her childhood, someone who had once been part of her world but whom she hadn't truly seen in years.

She turned to Pranav, her eyes sparkling with something deeper than nostalgia. "I've been here before. With friends, and with my parents. But never quite like this. It's strange, isn't it?" she said, her voice carrying a quiet joy that wasn't just about revisiting the past, but experiencing it with him.

The city, like the reunion itself, was more than what it had been in their memories. The way the past and present merged in that one moment was something new for her—this was no longer just Ameenabad from her memories. This was Ameenabad with Pranav, the childhood friend who had reentered her life after so long.

Pranav nodded, feeling the weight of her words. He had never been here before, not with Aparna, not with anyone. The faces of the people, the worn-out rickshaws, the narrow alleyways leading to small markets—it all seemed to blend into a dreamscape, something he had heard of but never quite experienced. For him, this was Ameenabad's first impression, and it was something profound, now tied to a reunion that felt like a rediscovery of self.

He looked at Aparna, her calm presence making the place seem less foreign.

Aparna smiled, a soft glint of enjoyment in her eyes. This was special—this visit, this city, and most importantly, sharing this moment with him, her childhood friend. Her memories of Ameenabad had always been tinged with nostalgia, but now, with Pranav, it felt like something was coming full circle.

This was a new beginning, a new chapter they were both writing together.

Pranav's gaze shifted, a hint of quiet realization in his eyes. "It's like we're meeting a part of our past for the first time," he murmured, almost to himself.

Ameenabad, at that moment, felt like a place caught between their shared childhood memories and the adults they had become. The old, fading buildings, the hum of voices, the sweetness of fried snacks—it was as though the city was waiting for them to discover it together, just as they were discovering themselves anew.

The warmth of the city mingled with the warmth of their shared moment, both of them holding on to the newness of the place, while Aparna felt the pull of familiarity, and Pranav stood at the crossroads of a memory he had yet to make.

The Ameenabad market hummed under the noon sun, its narrow streets bathed in warmth. Pranav, for the first time, felt the unfamiliarity of it all. He had never been here before, yet there was something oddly comforting in the bustle. The market's colors, the voices, the footsteps that stirred the dust—it felt like a place he should have known. But it was all foreign to him, a world he had only heard of in stories, a world Aparna had once been part of, and perhaps still was.

Aparna, however, was a part of it. She moved through the stalls as if she belonged, her hands brushing against bright fabrics and delicate chikan work with a kind of effortless grace. Her voice carried easily, weaving through the market's noise, telling stories of how she used to visit here, years ago, with friends and family.

"This one! This one's perfect!" she said, holding up a light pink kurti. The embroidery seemed to sparkle in the afternoon light. "Pranav, look at this! The way the white threads swirl around... It's so beautiful. Don't you think?"

Pranav's gaze shifted to the kurti, noticing the fine workmanship, but his thoughts weren't so much on the fabric. He watched her instead, the joy in her eyes as she spoke. He hadn't realized how much he missed this about her—the way she could find wonder in the smallest things. It was a quiet, simple pleasure, and yet, it was something that made her world feel alive.

"It's nice," he said, his words as soft as the warm air around them. There was a kind of stillness in his voice, something that matched his introspective nature. Shopping was never his thing, but seeing her so alive in the moment made it worthwhile.

Aparna, without missing a beat, handed the kurti to the shopkeeper, already chatting with him as she made her decision. She thought: This is going to be perfect for Lucknow. I'll wear it to Bada Imambada, for sure! Her expression was full of excitement, her eyes bright with anticipation as she pictured herself wearing it at the grand monument.

Pranav, still lost in the vibrancy of the market, wasn't exactly sure what to make of the place, but he watched her with quiet attention, her energy infecting him. He didn't need to speak much to understand her enthusiasm. She seemed at home here, surrounded by the familiar sights of Ameenabad, a place she had visited many times before, with friends, with family, and now with him.

As Aparna spoke to the shopkeeper, Pranav quietly stepped to the side. His eyes fell on a different kurti—one that he felt would suit her perfectly. The design wasn't extravagant, but the quality of the workmanship caught his attention. He turned to the shopkeeper and simply nodded. Without making a big deal of it, he paid for the kurti, though he didn't let on what he had done.

Aparna, still holding her purchase, turned back toward Pranav, adjusting the bag in her hands.

Pranav didn't answer immediately. He simply handed her the wrapped kurti with a quiet smile, his expression as reserved as ever, but his eyes soft.

Aparna paused for a moment, holding the package in her hands, a small smile crossing her face. "You got me something?" she asked, her voice a little surprised, but also warm with appreciation.

Without waiting for a response, she tore open the package and looked at the kurti. Her smile deepened as she glanced up at him.

"Thank you," she said quietly, a look of genuine appreciation in her eyes.

Pranav nodded, not needing to say much. It wasn't about the gift, but the thought behind it. As Aparna continued to smile, her fingers lightly touching the fabric, Pranav watched her with a quiet satisfaction, feeling that sense of connection deepen—in silence, just like the city around them.

They had wandered through every corner of Ameenabad, moving past fabric shops, golden bangles stacked high in glass cases, and sweet vendors pouring fresh syrup over piping hot jalebis. The lanes had been alive with chatter, the occasional honk of a cycle-rickshaw, and the rhythmic sound of a cobbler tapping on leather. It was a world that belonged to the everyday man—shopkeepers, customers, passersby—all woven into its timeless rhythm.

By the time they reached the Dhaba, hunger had set in. It was a modest place, the kind that didn't need a name. A thatched shade stretched over a few wooden tables, and an old ceiling fan creaked overhead. The air smelled of smoky tandoor, butter melting on hot rotis, and the earthy scent of lentils slow-cooked in brass pots.

They took their seats without a word. A middle-aged man with a towel draped over his shoulder, probably the owner, came over, wiping his hands on his kurta.

"What will you have?" he asked, as if the answer had always been obvious.

The food arrived soon after—dal makhni, paneer, rice, and butter roti, each dish steaming fresh. The paneer was soft and mildly spiced, the dal thick and creamy, the rotis crisp around the edges yet meltingly soft in the center. The meal required no conversation—just the quiet satisfaction that came from good food.

Halfway through his plate, Pranav lifted his hand slightly, catching the owner's attention. "Gulab jamun," he said.

Aparna, reaching for another piece of roti, paused. A slow smile crossed her lips, the kind that started subtly before taking over her face.

"You still remember?" she asked, her voice carrying a warmth that wasn't there a moment ago.

The Gulab jamun arrived in a shallow steel bowl, two golden-brown spheres floating in warm, fragrant syrup. The smell of caramelized sugar and cardamom filled the air.

Pranav broke a piece with his spoon, letting it soak a little longer before taking a bite. He didn't look at her when he spoke, but his words carried a quiet certainty.

"Some things never change."

Aparna leaned forward slightly, resting her elbow on the table, her expression thoughtful. There was something about the way he had said it—not teasing, not sentimental, just a simple truth.

She twirled the spoon in her fingers before finally taking a bite. The first taste brought back a hundred memories, some clear, some blurred by time. She glanced at him, a playful glint in her eyes.

"You really do know me well," she said, her voice dipping into something softer, something that wasn't quite a question, but wasn't just a statement either.

Pranav didn't reply. He simply nudged the bowl slightly toward her—an unspoken invitation.

The street outside continued as it always had—vendors called out their prices, a cycle-rickshaw wheeled past, a group of schoolboys laughed as they passed by. The world moved in its usual way.

But here, in this small Dhaba, amidst the scent of ghee and the clatter of steel plates, something else lingered—a moment unrushed, unspoken, but understood.

The evening light had softened, casting a mellow glow over the streets of Lucknow. The day had been long, filled with voices, colors, and the scent of old marketplaces. Now, as the city began to wind down, the streets carried a slower rhythm—shopkeepers counting their earnings, tea vendors pouring the last few cups, cycle-rickshaws making their final rounds.

The scooty hummed along the road, carrying its riders through the familiar paths of the city. It had been through a lot today—twisting through busy lanes, stopping near a crowded Dhaba, waiting patiently outside shops while bargains were made and laughter spilled over conversations. Now, it moved steadily, its tires rolling over well-worn roads, tracing the same routes it had known for years.

Pranav sat behind Aparna, the air now cooler, the city quieter. He didn't speak, but he didn't need to. The day had left its imprint—the sounds, the streets, the memories. He had never thought much about Ameenabad before, but now, it felt different. Maybe it wasn't the place. Maybe it was just the company.

They reached his stop. Aparna tapped the scooty's handle lightly, a casual gesture, but it felt almost like a signal—as if passing on an unspoken farewell.

Pranav stepped off. The scooty trembled for a brief second, as if impatient to move again.

Then, without ceremony, it sped off into the night, weaving back into the streets of Lucknow, as if it had more places to be, more stories to witness.

Its hum lingered in the air, fading into the distance, but leaving behind a quiet promise.

"Tomorrow, we ride again."

CHAPTER 8

The next morning arrived wrapped in the scent of damp earth. The streets still glistened with the remnants of the monsoon, puddles reflecting the early sunlight like scattered mirrors. The air was thick with warmth, yet softened by a playful breeze that carried the aroma of frying samosas and fresh rabri. The city was awake, alive, its rhythm unhurried yet constant.

Pranav adjusted his sleeves as he walked beside Aparna. He wasn't sure if the warmth on his face was from the lingering humidity or something else entirely. He stole a glance at her, only to find her already absorbed in their surroundings.

The rickshaws rattled past, their pullers wiping sweat off their brows with the ends of their gamchas. Vendors called out their prices, glass bangles shimmered under the sun, chikankari dupattas swayed in the breeze, and brass miniatures lined the stalls. Somewhere in the distance, a chaiwala's rhythmic pouring of tea into earthen cups blended into the melody of the street.

Yet, for Pranav, everything around him blurred into the background. His attention was drawn only to one thing—the girl walking beside him.

She wore a white chikankari kurti over dark blue jeans— effortless, simple, yet carrying an unshaken grace. There was no dupatta draped over her shoulders, no jewelry adorning her, yet she needed none. Her hair, dark and untamed, danced slightly with the wind, shifting ever so slightly before settling again. There was a quiet elegance in the way she walked—light, unhurried, as if she belonged here, as if the space around her had been waiting for her.

As Pranav followed her gaze, something inside him stirred. The towering arches, the layered domes, the carved details—they were grand, timeless, built to stand against the passage of years. And as he looked back at Aparna, he realized—she was the same.

She wasn't merely admiring the Bada Imambada. She was reflecting it.

The grand arches, sculpted with patience, stood unmoved, their presence commanding without trying. And in Aparna's stance, he saw the same effortless strength, the quiet confidence of something built to last. The smooth curves of the domes found their echo in the way her shoulders arched, her form rising with an ease that felt both delicate and unwavering.

Her face, unembellished, carried a glow—not stark, not loud, but the kind that lingered, much like the sunlight that fell on weathered sandstone.

And then there were her eyes.

Pranav's gaze lingered.

There was something about them—deep, layered, shifting like winding corridors, leading into spaces unknown. To look into them was to step into something infinite, something vast. They were not just eyes; they were a passage into another world, an intricate maze, a place one could enter but never fully understand.

Just like a labyrinth.

Just like Bhool Bhulaiya.

The corridors of her gaze stretched endlessly—some turns led into warmth, some into quiet mystery, and some into something so unknowable that one could only lose themselves further. There was no fixed path, no clear destination—only an invitation to wander deeper, to follow one turn after another, to keep searching without ever knowing if the way out would be found.

She turned slightly, and for a fleeting moment, the illusion of symmetry broke—only to return again in the next second, shifting, realigning, creating a new pattern just as the mind thought it had grasped the last.

Pranav had always heard stories of spaces designed to confound and mesmerize, of staircases leading nowhere, of walls that whispered secrets. But now, looking at her, he wondered if the real Bhool Bhulaiya was not built of stone and archways—but of a single glance, of a pair of eyes that held too many turns, too many pathways, too many secrets.

Could one ever find a way out of them?

Did one even want to?

Inside, the world seemed to disappear. The air turned cooler, thick with a silence that felt alive, as if the walls themselves were listening. Their footsteps echoed; their presence absorbed into the grandeur around them.

Aparna paused, placing a hand lightly against the stone. "Did you hear that?" she asked, her voice barely above a whisper.

Pranav listened. He had read about whispering galleries, about how a single murmur could travel through unseen corners. But hearing it now was different.

Aparna leaned in, her voice barely a breath against the stone. "These walls have ears."

A second later, her words returned to them from somewhere unseen, reshaped, softer, almost as if the space itself was answering her.

Pranav turned sharply, caught off guard. She only smiled, her eyes reflecting the quiet amusement of someone who had already known what to expect. "Amazing, isn't it?" she said.

He nodded, though his mind was elsewhere. "Yes… these walls do listen."

But as he looked at her, watching the way her lips curved in silent triumph, he wondered if he had been speaking of the place at all.

The staircase to the rooftop was narrow, spiraling upward as if leading to something beyond time itself. The stone steps, worn smooth by years of history, carried them higher until they emerged into the open sky. Below them, the city stretched endlessly— rooftops stacked like puzzle pieces, domes rising like silent witnesses, minarets standing still, watching over the passage of time.

Aparna stood at the edge, her hands resting on the old stone railing. The wind played with her hair again, teasing strands of it across her face before she absentmindedly tucked them away. She didn't move beyond that. She simply stood there, looking, as though she were absorbing the vastness rather than just seeing it.

Pranav watched her. It wasn't the city that held his gaze. It was her—the way she fit into it, the way she stood against the sky as if she belonged to it just as much as it belonged to her.

She turned to him, her eyes reflecting the brightness around them. "It's beautiful, isn't it?"

Pranav nodded. But he wasn't sure if he was agreeing with her or with something else entirely.

Because in that moment, looking at her, he understood something—some things weren't meant to be captured. They were meant to be felt. To be remembered.

Like the city. Like the sky. Like her.

As they made their way back down, the silence between them was not empty—it was filled with something unspoken, something neither of them needed to say. At the final turn, Aparna glanced back at him.

"You walk differently now."

Pranav raised an eyebrow. "How so?"

She shrugged, a teasing glint in her eyes. "Like someone carrying something invisible."

He didn't answer immediately. He let the words settle before saying, "Maybe I am."

She didn't ask what he meant, and he didn't explain. Some things were not meant to be spelled out. They sat quietly in the mind, like a conversation overheard from another room—recognizable, yet just out of reach.

The city welcomed them back, its rhythm unchanged. But for Pranav, something had shifted.

Aparna started her scooty, slipping effortlessly back into the streets, as if she had never paused at all. He watched as she rode away, disappearing into the lanes of Lucknow. But something lingered—an unfinished thought, a quiet realization that sat just beyond words.

Tomorrow would come, bringing its own rhythm, its own moments. But for now, this would remain—unspoken, unshaken, quietly alive in the spaces left between.

CHAPTER 9

The Shatabdi Express pulled out of Lucknow station at 3:30 PM, its wheels gliding smoothly over the tracks, leaving the city behind. Pranav adjusted himself in his seat by the window, his fingers tapping idly against the armrest. The familiar hum of the train, the rhythmic sway of the compartments—it all felt familiar, yet something inside him felt changed.

As Lucknow receded into the distance, Pranav found himself replaying the past few days. The streets of Ameenabad, the grandeur of the monument, the hushed corridors where voices lingered longer than they should. Aparna's voice, ever lively, filled his thoughts—the way she narrated stories of her city, her enthusiasm when pointing out something seemingly ordinary, her way of making the old feel new. He could almost hear her laugh over the quiet murmur of the train compartment.

Outside, the fields stretched endlessly, the occasional town flickering past in the setting sun. Passengers settled into their evening routines—some engrossed in newspapers, others staring at their phones, a few already dozing off. But Pranav remained still, his gaze fixed outside, lost in thoughts that refused to fade.

By the time the train reached New Delhi, the station buzzed with movement at 10 PM. Porters hurried along with luggage carts, families reunited with weary travelers, and auto drivers called out for passengers. Pranav stepped out, inhaling the distinct scent of the capital—a blend of dust, petrol, and the faint aroma of food from a nearby stall. He maneuvered through the crowd, making his way to the auto stand, haggled briefly over the fare, and soon found himself on his way home.

The city rushed past, familiar yet oddly distant. Towering streetlights, honking cars, and flickering neon signs—all remained the same as when he had left.

At exactly 10:45 PM, he stepped into the government-D-II type flat allotted to his father. The door creaked open, and his mother appeared, her face lit up with the quiet relief of a mother whose child has returned safely. She didn't say much—just a simple, "Aa gaye?" to which he nodded. His father was asleep, the living room dimly lit by the flickering glow of the television left on at low volume. His younger brother, already in their shared room, had curled up on the bed, fast asleep.

Pranav entered quietly, careful not to wake him. The familiarity of the room settled around him—the same old cupboard, the study table pushed against the wall, the faint scent of old books mingling with the night air. He placed his bag down, stretched his tired limbs, and collapsed onto the bed. A sigh escaped his lips, a quiet acceptance of being home.

His fingers reached for his phone. First, a quick message to Bua: "Reached." Then, almost instinctively, he typed another message to Aparna—just a simple acknowledgment.

Five minutes later, his phone buzzed. He opened the message, and a small, involuntary smile played on his lips.

Dear, that's great! See you soon! Good night, dear… bye… oops, sorry… We will meet again ☺

He stared at the words for a moment, rereading them as if trying to decipher something hidden between the lines. Then, without replying, he placed the phone on the bedside table, turned onto his side, and let his eyes close.

Somewhere, beyond the city lights, beyond the hum of another ordinary night, something remained—a thought, a memory, a quiet anticipation of what was yet to come.

CHAPTER 10

Two months had passed, slipping away quietly like an old newspaper carried off by the wind.

The morning sun fell lazily over the streets of Lajpat Nagar, where cycles rattled past hurried pedestrians, street vendors arranged fresh vegetables, and office-goers weaved through footpaths like they had rehearsed the route a thousand times.

Pranav walked past tea stalls and newspaper vendors; his bag slung over his shoulder. The office was only a few minutes away, but his mind was elsewhere—stuck between a conversation from the night before and the lingering presence of a name he couldn't shake away.

Aparna.

A blaring car horn snapped him back. He adjusted his bag strap, climbed the stairs, and pushed open the office door.

Inside, the day had already begun at its usual sluggish pace. The ceiling fan groaned in slow rotations, throwing uneven shadows on the walls. The printer had given up mid-job, coughing out a half-printed document before falling silent. The telephone rang intermittently, its shrill urgency ignored. Files were scattered across desks—some opened, others waiting for attention.

Anil Ji sat in his usual chair by the window, sipping chai, watching the office with the quiet patience of someone who had seen its best years fade into just another name on a door.

"This firm," he muttered to no one in particular, "could have been one of the biggest in the city."

Pranav glanced up. "How?"

Anil Ji smirked, tapping his chai cup. He had told this story before, but like an old habit, he indulged again.

"1955. Sir's father started this place. A wooden desk, a dream, and before anyone realized, it became a powerhouse—a name people trusted." He took another sip. "Then egos clashed. Partnerships broke. Clients left. What could have been legendary became… this."

The ceiling fan nodded in slow agreement.

The wooden door creaked open.

Nikhil Jain—better known as Nikhil Sr.—burst in, breathless, clutching a tax file like a man holding together a sinking ship.

"Bhai, yeh tax form galat ho gaya!" he announced, breathless, dropping the file onto Pranav's desk. "Meri articleship khatre mein hai!"

The ceiling fan groaned louder, unimpressed.

Pranav had seen this scene before—many, many times.

He sighed, flipping open the file with the same patience a doctor has when listening to a hypochondriac patient.

Before he could respond, the door opened again, this time with deliberate slowness.

Vikas Garg entered at his usual pace—unhurried, elegant, and with the calm confidence of a man who had never once rushed for anything in life. His tie was perfectly adjusted, his hair immaculately combed, and his expression one of faint disinterest.

"Sssar… traffic bohot tha!" he announced, his totla speech turning his excuse into something unintentionally amusing.

The wall clock, still frozen at 8:52 AM, remained unimpressed.

Nikhil Sr., still distressed about his tax file, paid no attention to him.

A few moments later, Vaibhav and Nikhil Kapoor (Nikhil Jr.) entered together, far quieter than the others.

Unlike Vikas or Nikhil Sr., they did not believe in grand entrances. They slipped into their seats with the quiet efficiency of people who preferred actions over words, picking up their work as though they had never left.

And just like that, the office was fully awake.

The rhythmic tapping of keyboards mixed with the soft murmurs of discussions. The smell of fresh tea from the pantry seeped into the air, blending with the scent of ink and aged paper.

And then, suddenly, the atmosphere shifted.

The office boy, Mukesh, straightened from his usual slouched position near the doorway. He squinted through the glass panel, his face growing serious.

He cleared his throat and, in a voice that was both grave and practiced, whispered the two words that sent shivers down every article's spine.

"Sir aa gaye!"

In an instant, everything transformed.

The casual murmurs disappeared. The scattered files were straightened. Pens were poised over notebooks. Computer screens, which had moments ago been showing news articles and cricket scores, suddenly displayed important financial reports.

Vikas, who had been leaning back lazily, sat up with forced concentration.

Nikhil Sr. stopped panicking about his tax file and picked up a pen, pretending to be deep in calculations.

Pranav, unlike the others, did not need to pretend. His file was already open, his pen already moving.

The door swung open.

CA Praveen Kumar Gupta stepped inside, adjusting his glasses, his sharp gaze sweeping the room.

He stood for a moment, his expression unreadable.

The office sat frozen in disciplined silence.

Even Anil Ji, who rarely cared for such dramatics, lifted his chai cup with an air of practiced nonchalance, taking another slow sip.

A long pause.

"Continue your work," CA Sir finally said.

The office collectively exhaled.

And thus, another day at the firm began.

The office settled into its usual rhythm, the clicking of keyboards blending with the faint hum of the ceiling fan, which seemed to be working harder than anyone in the room. Files shuffled, pens scratched against paper, and calculators performed their silent computations.

CA Praveen Kumar Gupta sat at his desk, reviewing a ledger, his glasses slipping slightly down the bridge of his nose. The room held its breath, waiting for the moment he would push back his chair.

Then, it happened.

He adjusted his wristwatch, gathered a few important files, and stood up. Without a word, he walked toward the door. The office followed his every movement, pretending to be immersed in work but stealing glances as he exited.

Mukesh, the office boy, stationed himself near the doorway, keeping an ear open for what had now become the most important announcement of the day.

The door closed behind CA Sir.

Mukesh waited a few seconds—just to be sure.

Then, turning to the room with the theatrical precision of a seasoned actor, he cleared his throat and whispered the words that caused an instant transformation.

"Sir chale gaye!"

The reaction was immediate.

Nikhil Sr. dropped his pen and let out a deep sigh, as though he had just survived a life-threatening ordeal. Vaibhav stretched his arms, shaking off the stiffness of morning discipline.

Vikas, who had been pretending to type something important, leaned back instantly, grinning. "F-finally! W-w-work mode off!"

Nikhil Jr., who had spent the last half hour staring at a blank Excel sheet, pulled out his headphones with a dramatic flick. "Ab toh vibe set karni padegi!"

Vaibhav smirked. "Aaj record bana diya. Poore do ghante bina bakwas ke kaam kiya tum logon ne."

Vikas grinned, running a hand through his neatly combed hair. "Ka-kaam kiya? Kis-kisne kiya?"

Before anyone could respond, Nikhil Sr. gasped dramatically.

"Arre bhai! Tax form ka adjustment galat ho gaya!" He grabbed his head in both hands, his eyes wide with panic. "Agar assessment officer ne pakad liya toh?"

Pranav, who had been flipping through his own file, barely glanced up and said in his calm Lucknowi tone, "Arey bhai, zyada tension mat lijiye. Sab dekh lenge. Abhi tak toh ek bhi client ko assessment notice nahi aaya."

Nikhil Sr. pointed at the form as though it was a crime scene. "Penalty! Fine! Career barbaad!"

Pranav sighed, adjusting his chair. "Arey bhai, pehle dekhiye toh sahi… aap har cheez pe ghabra jaate hain!"

Vikas chuckled, resting his chin on his hand. "Waise Nikhil bhaiya, aapko kisi ne bataya nahi kya? Yeh sab sirf first-time articles ke liye hota hai. Senior log bas MBS se kaam karwate hain aur tension free ho jaate hain!"

Pranav smirked, looking at Vikas. "Toh iska matlab aap bhi MBS ke sahare baithe hain?"

Vikas grinned nervously. "B-bhaiya, hum toh p-pichhle janam se aapke sahara hain!"

Even Anil Ji, who had been quietly sipping his second chai, smirked. "Nikhil, aap file theek se dekh lijiye. Agar galti hai toh MBS ko dikha dijiye."

The moment he said it, the room burst into laughter.

MBS.

It had started months ago when Pranav had once solved a tax mess-up with such confidence that Nikhil Sr. had jokingly said,

"Bhai, tu toh apna Guru Kant Desai hai!" (referring to Abhishek Bachchan's character from the movie Guru, known for his ambitious rise in business).

But it was Vikas, in his younger, playful tone, who had turned it into a nickname.

"M-MBS b-bhaiya!" he had called out one day. "Maanu Bhai Sharma! Jo kuch bhi sambhal lega!"

Since then, the name had stuck.

Vikas, looking up to Pranav as the firm's unofficial leader, grinned and clapped a hand on Nikhil Sr.'s shoulder. "Articles toh bahut aate hain, par MBS ek hi hai!"

Nikhil Sr. shook his head dramatically and sighed, "Bas bhai, ab se MBS ki tarah confidence loonga!"

Pranav smirked, leaned back in his chair, and in his signature Guru-style confidence, said: "Bhai, ye jo confidence aaya hai na, bahut mehnat se aaya hai. Manu Bhai jaisa confidence lena ho to Manu Bhai bankar lijiye, par yaad rahe—Manu Bhai ek hi hai!"

The room erupted into laughter.

The crisis—if one could even call it that—was resolved.

The office no longer resembled a place of work. Until Mukesh froze again.

"Sir wapas aa rahe hain!"

The illusion of productivity returned in seconds.

The door opened.

CA Sir glanced around. "Good. Carry on."

And just like that, masti time was over.

CHAPTER 11

Meanwhile, in a parallel world, while Pranav's office hummed with the rapid clicking of keyboards and the occasional burst of laughter from his colleagues, Aparna found herself in a very different environment—one where time seemed to move at a more measured, almost lethargic pace.

The training center was located in a quiet town nestled between rolling hills and old colonial buildings. The air had a crispness to it, a refreshing contrast to the usual city smog. The institute, responsible for shaping future probationary officers, was a sprawling campus with structured schedules and rigorous sessions. A mix of old government-style architecture and modern classrooms made up the space, with glass-panel windows reflecting the golden hues of the morning sun. A neatly maintained garden lined the pathways, though few trainees ever paid attention to it in their hurry to reach the lecture halls.

Aparna arrived five minutes before the session was set to begin. She had quickly learned that punctuality was a relative concept at the training center. The instructor was rarely on time, and when he was, the first ten minutes were reserved for him adjusting his chair, clearing his throat, and shuffling his notes as though they had been mysteriously rearranged overnight.

She took her usual seat—third row from the front, near the window, where a soft breeze occasionally found its way in. The room, though large, had the uncanny ability to feel stuffy within minutes. A ceiling fan spun overhead, creaking rhythmically, as though protesting its own existence. The windows, though generously sized, let in just enough sunlight to remind everyone of the world outside but not enough to make them feel like they were part of it.

The other trainees trickled in slowly. There was Meenal, who always carried an extra notebook but never wrote in it, and Ashish, whose single objective in training seemed to be securing a seat nearest to the air cooler. A few others exchanged lazy greetings before settling down. The classroom buzzed with quiet murmurs, the sound of pages being flipped, and the occasional clatter of a dropped pen.

The instructor entered precisely twelve minutes late, clearing his throat twice before addressing the class.

"Good morning," he announced, peering over his spectacles. "Today, we will discuss customer handling and grievance redressal. A very important topic."

Aparna listened attentively, though the heat in the room made concentration feel like an endurance test. The instructor spoke in a slow, deliberate manner, occasionally pausing to emphasize a point that no one would remember by the end of the day.

"The key," he continued, "is patience. The customer is always— well, usually—right."

There was a faint chuckle from the back of the room. Even the instructor smirked slightly before regaining his composure.

The lecture stretched on, broken occasionally by a question from a particularly earnest trainee or the dull ring of someone's phone, which was immediately silenced under the instructor's sharp gaze.

By the time lunch break arrived, the trainees spilled out into the corridor like schoolchildren freed from class. Aparna found a seat on the bench outside, where a small breeze relieved the weight of the afternoon heat. She pulled out her phone, scrolling absentmindedly through messages. There it was—Pranav's message from earlier in the day.

She hesitated for a moment before opening it again, rereading his words twice. A small smile played on her lips as she quickly typed a reply and hit send. The phone screen dimmed, and she placed it aside, exhaling softly.

The training was important, she reminded herself, but there were moments when it all felt like a rehearsal for something far bigger, something that would only begin once she stepped into the real world.

After lunch, the classroom regained its sluggish rhythm. The instructor continued his lesson, now shifting to banking regulations. The room, already warm, seemed to lull everyone into a dazed state. Ashish, despite all his efforts to stay alert, nodded off briefly before jolting awake and pretending to write something important. Even Meenal, the most diligent of the lot, had begun to doodle in her untouched notebook.

Aparna, fighting the same sluggishness, rested her chin on her hand, staring blankly at the board. The instructor droned on about compliance measures, his voice blending into the background hum of the fan. It was during one of these moments—where time seemed to stretch endlessly—that the class was suddenly jolted awake.

The instructor, after a brief pause, looked around and called out, "Miss Aparna, can you repeat the last point?"

Aparna blinked, sat up straight, and glanced at her notebook.

There was no last point.

She hadn't written anything.

A few heads turned toward her.

She cleared her throat, pretending to scan the page, and then, with an air of confidence, said, "The... uh... process should be handled with utmost diligence and accuracy."

The instructor raised an eyebrow.

It was a vague answer. It could have applied to any topic—from loan verification to washing vegetables properly.

But he nodded anyway.

Satisfied, Aparna let out a silent breath and returned to her previous task—waiting for the session to end.

As the day drew to a close, Aparna stretched her arms and gathered her books. The room emptied gradually, trainees leaving in pairs or small groups, their conversations light and easy. She lingered a moment longer, enjoying the quiet that came once the chatter had faded.

CHAPTER 12

The next day arrived wrapped in a soft morning mist, the air crisp with the scent of damp earth and freshly brewed chai from roadside stalls. The quiet town stirred to life in its usual, unhurried rhythm—scattered footsteps on damp pathways, the occasional rickshaw passing by, and the distant toll of a school bell marking the hour. Aparna stretched, embracing the calm before the day unfolded.

Mornings, she believed, were neither good nor bad—it all depended on how well one dressed for them. And Aparna never got that part wrong. Today, she picked a deep green cotton kurti, embroidered with fine floral motifs—subtle, yet striking, like a touch of poetry woven into fabric. A cream-colored churidar softened the look, its delicate folds moving with effortless grace. A pair of simple silver earrings, elegant yet understated, completed her look as she tied her hair into a loose braid—practical, yet charming in a way only she could manage.

As she stepped outside, the morning chill lingered in the air, and the quiet streets stretched ahead in familiar patterns. The road to the training center was as predictable as ever—past the silent bookshops, the tall school buildings with aging colonial facades, and the neatly arranged gardens lining the institute's entrance. Just before reaching the gate, she paused, slipped her hand into her bag, and pulled out her Nokia 1100.

With practiced ease, she typed:

Good morning, dear! Hope your calculator isn't as confused as you are in the morning 😲 *How are you?*

A moment later, she hit Send, slipped the phone into her bag, and let a small, knowing smile touch her lips. The message had been delivered, but it would take its own time to be read. She slipped the phone back into her bag and stepped inside the training center, disappearing into the day's rhythm—just as she had the morning before.

The message left Aparna's Nokia 1100 with quiet determination, slipping into the unseen web of signals stretching across cities. It bounced from one tower to the next, like a letter hopping across postboxes, each relay taking it closer to its destination.

It soared over highways, slipped past railway tracks, and finally entered the restless heart of New Delhi, where the pace was faster, the air heavier, and the mornings never quite as gentle. It arrived at its intended stop—Pranav's Nokia 2280, resting quietly on his office desk, surrounded by files, calculators, and half-filled notepads.

The phone screen blinked, the tiny green light pulsing patiently, waiting to be seen. But Pranav was busy, flipping through a ledger with the focus of a man who had long accepted that balance sheets demanded more attention than his personal life.

Across from him, Nikhil Jr. leaned back in his chair, spinning a pen between his fingers—watching, waiting, always ready to pounce at the slightest distraction.

The message remained unread, but not unnoticed.

The tiny green signal blinked like a child tugging at a distracted parent's sleeve. But Pranav, immersed in numbers, remained oblivious.

Across the desk, Nikhil Jr., the youngest and most restless article in the office, had been watching. Not openly, of course—experience had taught him that curiosity worked best when disguised. He leaned back, twirling his pen, pretending to focus on a tax computation while his sharp eyes flickered toward Pranav's still-blinking phone.

And then, it happened.

A brief pause in work, a subconscious stretch of the arms, and Pranav finally picked up the phone. His thumb hovered over the keypad before pressing the familiar buttons—one, two, three clicks—and the message opened.

Good morning, dear! Hope your calculator isn't as confused as you are in the morning 😵 *How are you?*

For a split second, the edges of Pranav's lips curled upward—small, fleeting, the kind of smile one doesn't plan, the kind that simply escapes.

And that was all Nikhil Jr. needed.

"Aha!" he declared triumphantly, leaning forward with the energy of a detective solving his first big case. "Caught you!"

Pranav, startled, snapped the phone shut—too late to hide his reaction.

"What?" he asked, attempting nonchalance.

But Nikhil Jr. had already seen everything—the smile, the name, the unmistakable warmth in Pranav's expression. He grinned, tapping a finger against the desk as if summoning the confession he knew was coming.

"Aparna," he said slowly, savoring the name like a well-kept secret finally unearthed. "Now, tell me, bhaiya… who is she?"

Pranav didn't hesitate. He never did.

"She is my childhood friend," he said, his voice steady, matter-of-fact. "We met on a train after twelve years."

Nikhil Jr.'s eyebrows shot up. "That's it?"

Pranav nodded. "That's it." He paused for a beat before adding, "And I think I have feelings for her."

That caught Nikhil Jr.'s full attention. "Oh?"

Pranav exhaled. "But you know I'm bad at expressing."

Nikhil Jr. sat back, absorbing this information. And then, without warning, he dramatically leaned back in his chair, flicked an imaginary scarf, and, in the most exaggerated SRK style, declared—

"Bhaiya, Mai hoon na!"

Pranav gave him a blank stare. "What?"

"I am here!" Nikhil Jr. declared. "I will handle this! I will make sure you reply in a way that makes her feel something!"

Pranav sighed. "It's just a message."

"No," Nikhil Jr. said, shaking his head. "A tax return is just a message. This? This is life!"

Pranav shook his head, muttering something about people taking SMS conversations too seriously, but before he could protest further, Nikhil Jr. had already grabbed a pen and was making notes.

At last, Pranav typed out the final message:

If calculators could think, mine would have resigned long ago 😄
I'm good. Hope you had a great day!

He hovered over the send button.

Nikhil Jr. nodded seriously. "Do it."

Pranav pressed send.

The phone beeped. The message was gone.

Miles away, in a quiet room dimly lit by the glow of a small bedside lamp, Aparna's phone vibrated.

(Sent at 4:12 PM. Delivered at 9:43 PM. The telecom gods had their reasons.)

She reached for it, rubbing her eyes as she turned it over and pressed the button.

If calculators could think, mine would have resigned long ago 😅 *I'm good. Hope you had a great day!*

She stared at it for a second. Then, without meaning to, she smiled.

It wasn't just a reply. It is his reply. And that made all the difference.

Placing the phone beside her pillow, she let her eyes close, the words lingering in the quiet.

Within minutes, she drifted off to sleep, the faint glow of the screen fading into darkness

CHAPTER 13

November arrived with a quiet sense of urgency. The air still carried the fading warmth of Diwali, but for Pranav, celebrations had been reduced to a distant hum outside his window. His world, for now, was made up of accounting standards, tax laws, and endless revisions.

His leave had started, a rare luxury in articleship life, meant only for those braving the CA exams. The Professional Competence Course (PCC) was no joke—six exams spread across eleven days, each one designed to squeeze every ounce of reasoning out of a candidate. The first exam was scheduled right after Diwali, adding an extra layer of difficulty.

While the city lit up with fireworks and laughter, Pranav's room was illuminated only by the soft glow of his study lamp. A balance sheet in one hand and a calculator in the other, he trudged through concepts he had revised more times than he cared to count.

Each morning of the exam days, his phone played its small but significant role. It would light up at almost the same time with a message from Aparna—simple, predictable, yet comforting.

All the best, Pranav! Hope you do well today 😊

It wasn't extravagant, but it had a certain reliability to it, like a familiar milestone on an otherwise endless road.

Pranav read each message, smiled, and tucked the phone away before heading off to battle another paper.

But on the last exam day, the message never came.

For the first time in eleven days, his phone sat idle, not buzzing with its usual words of encouragement. He noticed the silence but said nothing. Perhaps she was busy. He picked up his pen, walked into the exam hall, and let the thought drift away—only to resurface later when the final paper was done, when relief had started to sink in.

That evening, as he returned home, the silence was finally broken.

Hey Pranav, I'm really sorry for not messaging you earlier. I was caught up with on-site training and couldn't wish you. How did your exams go?

Pranav leaned back on his chair, a faint smile tugging at his lips. He typed his reply:

No worries, Aparna! Exams went okay, but you know how it is. I'll clear it, special friend's wishes are with me.

He hit send and watched as the message vanished into the unknown, like a paper boat drifting into a vast sea of networks, waiting to find its way to her.

Life at the office resumed as if nothing had changed. Pranav returned to his desk, picked up pending files, and rejoined the rhythm of balance sheets and tax audits. But somewhere in between, his phone continued to play its part—buzzing every now and then with messages from Aparna.

How's everything going? Hope the office is keeping you busy. Did you get time to relax after the exams?

Yeah, back to the grind. Busy as usual, but it's all good. How's your training going?

I'm surviving on coffee and sheer willpower! But don't worry, I'll make it through 😵

Their conversations weren't long, but they had a certain rhythm now, like the casual exchange of words between old friends who knew exactly where to pick up from.

Days passed.

One evening, Pranav thought about calling Aparna. He stared at his phone, thumb hovering over the call button. But then, like a whispered warning, he remembered something she had once said:

"My friends are upset with me because I don't pick up calls."

A joke, perhaps. But Pranav knew himself well enough—he wasn't the kind to take risks easily. He placed the phone down and did what he always did instead.

He turned on his PC, opened Orkut, and searched for her profile.

Orkut was a world of its own. A place where people left messages on each other's "scraps," where testimonials were written with excessive adjectives, and where friendships were measured in the number of community memberships.

Pranav scrolled through Aparna's profile, glancing at the pictures she had posted. There was something effortless about them—smiling in one, lost in thought in another. He hesitated before typing a comment under one of them.

You've always had an eye for the perfect moment.

A simple compliment. He clicked submit and leaned back, half expecting nothing, half hoping for a reply.

Later, when he checked, she had responded to others, but not him.

A small, familiar disappointment settled in. He shook it off, telling himself it didn't matter. But later that night, as he lay staring at the ceiling, he gave in and sent her a text.

I never get replies on Orkut...

Her response was immediate.

Oh, Orkut is for people far away... for those who live in your heart, there are messages!

Pranav read it once. Then again. And then, slowly, he smiled.

The next day at the office, he showed the message to Nikhil Jr.

"Look at this," he said, handing over his phone.

Nikhil Jr. read it once, then clutched the phone dramatically, as if he had just uncovered the greatest love story ever told.

"Bhaiya," he declared. "This is it. This is your moment. The heroine has delivered her dialogue; now it's time for the hero's response!"

Pranav frowned. "It's not a movie, Nikhil."

"It is," Nikhil Jr. insisted. "And lucky for you, you've got me— your personal love guru. Trust me, I'll handle this."

Before Pranav could protest, Nikhil Jr. had taken his phone and started typing. His fingers moved with the confidence of a man who had written love letters for half the office.

Finally, he handed the phone back.

Pranav read the message and felt his stomach turn.

If messages are for those who live in the heart, then I think I'd like to keep receiving yours forever.

He glanced up at Nikhil Jr. "You expect me to send this?"

"Of course!"

"It's too much."

"It's perfect."

Pranav hesitated. He had never been good at this. Expressing, feeling, saying things that mattered. His instinct was always to keep things simple, to hold back.

But then, before he could overthink it, Nikhil Jr. reached over and hit send.

"There," he said with satisfaction. "It's done."

Pranav's heart raced, but there was nothing to do now except wait.

Meanwhile, in a quiet room, Aparna sat on her bed, phone in hand, reading Pranav's message.

She smiled.

She placed her phone down, her heart fluttering slightly.

She smiled again, a romantic smile, something that spoke more than words ever could.

CHAPTER 14

January arrived with an air of quiet anticipation. The celebrations of the new year had settled, and now the weight of reality returned—CA results were just around the corner.

Pranav had never been one for dramatic displays of nervousness, but even he couldn't ignore the growing tension in the air. The days leading up to the result were filled with a mix of hope, anxiety, and forced distractions—a little more scrolling through messages than usual, a few more glances at his phone as if it held the answers before the Institute did.

Finally, the day arrived. The results were declared.

He checked.

First group—cleared.

Second group—missed by three marks.

Pranav stared at the screen, sighed, and leaned back in his chair. It was neither a complete failure nor a full victory—just a small, frustrating pause before the journey continued.

Later that evening, he typed a message to Aparna, choosing to laugh at the situation rather than dwell on it.

I failed in the last exam. Only reason—my special friend's wishes were not with me!

Aparna's reply came almost immediately.

Hey! That's not fair! I was there for all your other exams!

Pranav smiled.

Exactly. See what happened when you skipped the last one?

Hmm… point noted! Next time, I'll make sure I don't miss a single one!

She was happy for him, despite the partial success. In the flow of the conversation, she casually asked,

How much longer do you have to go for this course?

Pranav replied:

I have 1.5 years of articleship left, then the final exams. If everything goes well in the first attempt, I'll be done by May 2011.

Oh! That's a long way to go…

For a brief moment, Pranav considered leaving it at that, but something within him nudged him forward. Without overthinking, he typed:

If you're with me, this journey will feel shorter.

The moment the message was sent, he felt a familiar hesitation creep in—had he said too much?

But then, her reply came.

It wasn't direct. It wasn't dramatic.

But it was a confirmation.

A simple reply, yet one that carried more weight than the longest conversations.

The months passed in their usual rhythm—work, studies, conversations that never overstayed their welcome, yet always seemed to pick up right where they left off.

Then came March.

Pranav was visiting Lucknow again, and this time, he sent Aparna a message in advance.

I'll be in town on your birthday. Would be great to catch up!

She replied soon after.

Okay, we'll meet!

Pranav smiled to himself. This time, he would see her again after so many months.

He even bought a birthday card for her, something carefully chosen, not too formal, not too extravagant—just enough to say what he never quite found the words for.

But as fate would have it, things didn't go as planned.

Aparna got caught up with something unavoidable, and the meeting never happened.

That evening, his phone buzzed with her message.

I'm so, so sorry! I really wanted to meet, but I couldn't make it. Hope you understand.

Pranav stared at the unread message for a moment before typing back:

Of course. These things happen.

He didn't say much else. He didn't need to. The small weight of disappointment settled in his chest, but he shook it off. Life had a way of making plans and then laughing at them.

Aparna messaged again.

I'll come to Delhi to collect my birthday card from you!

Pranav smiled. A postponed meeting was still a meeting.

April arrived, and with it, Pranav's birthday.

The day itself was like any other. Work went on, messages poured in, a mix of well-wishers, colleagues, and old friends. But in the back of his mind, there was an expectation—a quiet, unspoken one.

Aparna would call.

He waited.

Morning passed. No message.

Afternoon. Still nothing.

By evening, the thought began to nudge at him—had she forgotten?

Finally, on impulse, he dialed her number.

The phone rang once.

And then, just as quickly, he cut the call.

What was he expecting? A grand gesture? A reminder? No, that wasn't him. This wasn't a scene from a movie, and he wasn't the kind to ask for attention.

Minutes passed.

Then, his phone rang.

He picked up.

"Why did you cut the call?" Aparna's voice came through, carrying a mix of curiosity and mild complaint.

"You said you don't pick up calls," he said, smiling faintly.

"That's not what I meant!" She sounded exasperated. "You should have just waited!"

For a moment, there was silence—not awkward, but comfortable, like a pause between familiar notes in a song.

Then Pranav said, "It's my birthday today."

Aparna gasped. "Oh no! I'm so sorry! I completely forgot!"

Before he could say anything else, she spoke again.

"Wait. One second."

And then, to his surprise, she started singing.

It was soft, unplanned, and yet, somehow perfect.

"Happy birthday to you… happy birthday to you…"

The song drifted through the call, her voice carrying a warmth that no message or card could ever match.

Pranav leaned back in his chair, listening, letting the moment settle.

When she finished, she laughed lightly. "That was terrible, wasn't it?"

Pranav shook his head, even though she couldn't see him. "No," he said quietly. "It was perfect."

They talked for a little while longer—nothing too deep, just casual conversation, a few jokes, and a reluctant goodbye.

But as Pranav placed his phone down, he realized something.

It wasn't the words.

It wasn't the message.

It was her voice.

After months of messages, after carefully chosen words and thoughtful pauses, he had heard her voice again.

And it was enough to make him realize—he had missed it more than he thought.

That night, as he lay awake, the memory of her voice lingered in his mind.

Perhaps it was just a call.

Perhaps it was just a song.

Or maybe, it was the beginning of something neither of them had put into words yet.

For now, he let the thought rest.

Some things were best left unsaid—until the time was right

CHAPTER 15

August had arrived without much ceremony, slipping into the year like a quiet guest. The days were steady, predictable—office work, study hours, and the occasional exchange of messages that had now become part of Pranav's routine.

By now, he had cleared his PCC exams and was fully focused on his CA final exams in May 2011. The journey ahead was long, but Pranav had learned to take it one step at a time.

The messages with Aparna remained unchanged—light, playful, and easy.

How's the studying going? she asked one day.

Going great! Just waiting for you to take my exam on my behalf.

Oh, sure! But you'll have to handle my training in return!

Deal!

And so, their exchanges continued—sometimes a joke, sometimes a simple check-in, always effortless.

Then came a Sunday afternoon, when the world outside moved lazily under the slow sun. The roads were quieter, the tea stalls less crowded, and even the air seemed to carry the weight of a weekend nap.

For reasons he couldn't explain, Pranav picked up his phone and dialed her number.

It rang once. Twice.

Then, she answered.

"Pranav?"

"Random call," he said casually.

Aparna laughed lightly. "I thought it was time I surprised you."

There was a pause. Not awkward, just the kind that made space for unspoken thoughts.

Then, without much thought, Pranav spoke.

"You know, I think I like you."

Aparna went silent for a moment, as if the words had reached her but had not yet settled.

"That's sweet, Pranav…" she finally said, her tone lighter than expected. "But there's something you should know—I'm Manglik. And a Manglik can only marry another Manglik."

Pranav sat up, processing the sudden shift from emotions to astrology.

"If that's the case," he said, "then I am the best match for you. My planetary position cancels out the Manglik dosh!"

Aparna burst into laughter. "You seem very sure about that."

"Of course! I might not know astrology, but I know one thing—I don't let technicalities get in the way of good things."

She was still laughing when she said, "You're impossible, Pranav."

"And you're predictable, Aparna. You always find a way to challenge me," he replied, grinning.

A few minutes later, Aparna casually changed the topic.

"You know, during my MBA, there was this guy named Girish…"

Pranav frowned slightly. "So, you liked him?"

Aparna didn't hesitate. "Yes, I did."

Pranav felt a shift—a small, barely noticeable discomfort settling in.

He kept his voice neutral. "I thought you liked me."

Aparna paused for a second before saying, "Of course, I like you, but we were in MBA."

Pranav leaned forward, his voice carrying mock indignation. "And what's my mistake in that?"

Aparna laughed. "It's not a mistake, Pranav. It's just… different."

"Different how?" he pressed.

"You and I—we have our own bond. Girish was just part of my MBA life."

Pranav sighed theatrically. "Great. That's just great. And here I was, thinking I had a chance!"

Aparna laughed. "He was just a classmate, Pranav. He studied MBA with me."

"And that," Pranav declared, "is hardly my fault! What was I supposed to do? Join MBA instead of CA just to compete with this Girish?"

Aparna giggled.

"In fact," Pranav continued, now on a roll, "the alphabets in our names are almost the same too! Only 'A' and 'V' are different!"

Aparna shook her head on the other end of the line, but she was still smiling.

"And let's be honest," Pranav added, "I'm sure this Girish doesn't even understand Tax Laws and Financial Management as well as I do!"

Aparna's laughter softened, and for a moment, she said nothing. Then, after a beat, her voice came through—quieter this time.

"Manu…"

There was something different in the way she said it—a weight to it, a softness, a familiarity that went beyond words.

Pranav didn't reply immediately. He let the silence stretch, feeling something settle in his heart.

Some conversations didn't need conclusions.

Some emotions didn't need explanations.

For now, this was enough.

Later that night, as Pranav lay on his bed, his phone vibrated. It was a message from Aparna.

Are you sad and angry?

Pranav stared at the screen for a moment before typing back.

No…

A moment later, he sent another message.

To be honest, yes.

There was no reply for a few minutes. Then, Aparna's response appeared.

I appreciate your honesty, Manu. But don't overthink things. It's good you're doing CA after all... Tax planning is the best!

Pranav read the message twice.

And then, without realizing it, he smiled.

Some words said more than they seemed to.

Some words were meant to be read twice.

Tonight, these were enough

CHAPTER 16

February arrived, wrapping the world in its familiar winter hush. The days remained crisp, the chill lingering in the air, while the nights, though still cold, had begun to surrender their length to the approaching spring. And life, as always, carried on in its usual, indifferent manner.

At the bank training center, Aparna was in the final stage of her training, inching closer to the next phase of her career. Meanwhile, in his world of ledgers and law books, Pranav was buried in preparations for his CA final exams, just three months away.

Yet, despite the weight of responsibilities pressing on both their shoulders, their exchanges remained unchanged—playful, effortless, never overstaying their welcome.

Then, one evening, without much thought, Pranav sent her a message.

I don't know what to call this, but I know one thing—life feels better when you're in it.

Aparna's reply came almost instantly.

Oh God, Pranav! Am I really that bad that everyone keeps proposing to me?

Pranav smirked. He could picture her rolling her eyes, shaking her head at the absurdity of it all.

No, no," he replied. You're not bad at all. You're a marriage product!

She took longer to respond this time, as if she were thinking before she typed.

Why do we have to complicate relationships, Pranav?

He stared at the screen for a moment before replying.

I'm a boy, Aparna. If I've developed feelings for you, how is that my fault?

Her response was brief.

Hmmm.

And then, silence.

Pranav had made up his mind.

For months, he had wrestled with his emotions, trying to convince himself that what he felt for Aparna was nothing more than friendship. But something about their conversations—the comfort in their words, the way he checked his phone just a little too often—told him otherwise.

That night, as he sat on his bed, staring at his phone, he knew he couldn't ignore it any longer.

The Nokia 2280 lay beside him, its tiny screen glowing faintly in the dim light.

It had been through too much.

It had delivered countless messages, stored more unsent drafts than he cared to admit, and had been a silent witness to every hesitation, every half-written confession that never saw the light of day.

And now, it was waiting.

Just like him.

His fingers lingered over the keypad for a moment before he began typing.

I've spent months trying to put this into words, but the truth is simple—I want you in my life, not just as a friend, but as someone I can share every moment with. Will you be mine?

He read it once.

Then once more.

His left hand held the phone steady, his thumb hovering over the send button, motionless.

His right hand stirred the Bournvita, the spoon clinking softly against the cup.

The warm liquid swirled lazily in slow, familiar circles.

And just like that, his mind slipped back.

The same swirling motion.

The same quiet night.

The same restless thoughts.

Except, it wasn't 2011 anymore.

The Bournvita had taken him back.

He was standing in the kitchen, the air thick with silence. The faint aroma of cardamom lingered, mixing with the slight dampness of an unfinished summer evening.

The spoon in his hand had stopped moving. The warmth of the cup remained, but his fingers felt cold.

Outside, the distant hum of a passing vehicle faded into the night. Somewhere, a clock ticked, indifferent to the moments it measured.

The Bournvita swirled, slower this time, reluctant—pulling him back, deeper, beyond the ache, beyond the questions, beyond the note that still trembled in his hands. And before he knew it, April 2003 unfolded—a time when friendships felt eternal, laughter came easy, and love had yet to leave its first scar.

The past had arrived, and it wasn't leaving anytime soon.

CHAPTER 17

The morning was refreshing beyond imagination. The air carried a crispness that felt new, almost as if the world had been washed clean overnight. The Bournvita had taken him here—not just to another time, but to another version of himself. A boy who had just finished his 12th Board exams three days ago, untethered from textbooks and deadlines, stepping into the world with nothing but time on his hands. Having read plenty about the benefits of morning walks, he had finally decided to give it a try. Little did he know, this quiet Sunday morning would mark the beginning of something he would remember forever.

As he entered the park, a cool breeze brushed against his face, carrying away the last traces of sleep. The Bournvita had brought him here, into this quiet morning, where the air smelled of fresh earth and forgotten stories. A chorus of birds welcomed him, their songs weaving through the rustling leaves. A gentle wind sent them floating down, one by one, carpeting the ground in golden brown. The park stretched before him, alive in its stillness, offering a kind of peace that made him feel, for the first time in days, truly awake.

For thirty minutes, the world had been nothing but the steady rhythm of footsteps, the quiet pulse of breath, and the soft crunch of gravel beneath running shoes. The morning stretched, golden and untouched, carrying the crispness of a day still unspoiled.

Then, the pace slowed.

Shoes slipped off.

The damp grass greeted bare feet with a cool embrace, the lingering dew clinging to the blades, shimmering like scattered pearls in the morning light. The ground felt softer, as if it had been waiting, as if it belonged only to this moment.

And then, the silence shifted.

A voice.

Soft, effortless—woven into the morning air like it had always been there. It wasn't loud, nor seeking attention—just a quiet tune, hummed absentmindedly, carried away by the breeze.

Steps faltered.

A few paces ahead, just near the curve of the path, walked a girl.

Only her back was visible at first—the way her long, wavy hair cascaded down, catching the sunlight in its strands, making them shimmer as she moved. She walked barefoot, her steps light, almost soundless, as if she belonged to the morning in a way nothing else did.

And then, a hesitation.

It was subtle—the briefest pause in movement, the slightest stillness in her steps, as if sensing something unseen.

Then, she turned.

For the first time, her face came into view.

The morning light touched her just right—soft, golden, painting her skin in warm hues. Her deep brown eyes, large and expressive, held something unreadable, a quiet curiosity that neither questioned nor revealed too much. They carried the kind of stillness that made time pause, like the hush before a whispered secret.

Her dark wavy hair, slightly tousled from the breeze, framed her face effortlessly, each strand catching the soft morning glow. It tumbled over her shoulders, moving with an easy grace, as if the wind itself had shaped it.

She wasn't wearing anything extravagant—just a simple, pastel-colored tracksuit, yet there was something about the way it sat on her frame that made it feel effortless. The fabric looked soft, welcoming, as if it carried the morning's chill within its folds. The sleeves were slightly long, half-covering her wrists, and when she moved, the fabric gathered loosely, adding to the quiet ease of her presence.

There was no rush in her expression. No urgency in the way she looked.

Just the faintest tilt of her lips—not quite a smile, not quite indifference—just something in between.

She wasn't looking at the sky.

She wasn't looking at the trees.

She was looking at him.

The moment stretched, weightless, suspended in something unspoken.

Then, a gust of wind stirred the trees. A few dry leaves drifted down, one brushing against a shoulder before settling on the grass.

And just like that, the spell was broken.

A sharp breath.

A heartbeat too loud.

Without a thought, without a reason, the feet turned—and ran.

The earth barely felt the hurried steps as they retreated. The quiet park stood undisturbed, watching as the moment slipped away.

It should have ended there.

But the next morning, it happened again.

And the next.

For days, the strange rhythm continued—arrival, the same voice, the same silhouette. And each time, as if by some silent pattern, she would pause, turn, and look.

And each time—without fail—he would run.

And then, one morning, the pattern broke.

The voice was there, the quiet humming threading through the air as always. The sunlight danced in familiar patterns on the dewy grass. The rhythm was unchanged—until something else entered the silence.

Laughter.

Not hers.

A few young boys, loitering near the park entrance, their voices low, their words carelessly strung together. Not loud enough to be direct, yet just enough to be heard. Their eyes flickered toward her, their smirks curling at the edges, waiting for a reaction.

He didn't think.

He just ran.

The dewy grass pressed against his bare feet as he closed the distance between them. Uninvited, unannounced—yet entirely certain that he belonged there in that moment.

He didn't look at her. Didn't say a word. He simply slowed his pace beside her, matching her steps as if it had always been this way.

She didn't react at first.

Just a brief glance, an unreadable expression. But there was no hesitation in her steps, no questioning gaze. Just acknowledgment.

Ahead, the voices hesitated.

A moment of uncertainty passed between them before one of the boys nudged the other, murmured something under his breath, and with a casual shrug, they turned and left.

The park belonged to the morning once more.

For the first time, they walked together.

No words.

Just the quiet sound of footsteps on damp earth.

The walking track had never felt this long before.

The silence wasn't uneasy, nor was it familiar—it was new. Like the first page of a book, waiting for the story to begin. A sideways glance—hesitant, quick, as if testing the weight of this newfound presence.

No reaction.

No question of why or how.

Just a step forward, and another, and another.

As if this had always been the way things were meant to be.

And then, just as the path curved toward the exit, she broke the silence.

"You run too much."

The words were light, laced with amusement.

For a second, he wasn't sure if he had actually heard them.

She turned slightly, looking at him—not waiting for a response, not expecting one. Then, as if the moment was already slipping away, she added casually, "I'm Trapta."

A name.

Offered simply. Easily. As though it was just another piece of the morning, floating into the air with the dewdrops and the rustling leaves.

Nine, maybe ten years had passed, yet this was the first time that name was heard—spoken aloud, offered without hesitation.

Despite living in the same government quarters all these years—her on the sixth floor, him on the second—this was the first time the invisible walls of familiarity had broken.

For years, they had existed within the same walls, the same staircases, the same corridors. Yet today was the first time they truly existed for each other.

CHAPTER 18

The days stretched ahead, unchanging, yet carrying within them a quiet anticipation. The morning air held a familiar chill, and the streets stirred with the same early footsteps. And amidst it all, a silent pattern began to take shape.

At the same hour each morning, two figures stepped out—their breaths forming misty whispers in the dawn, their footsteps merging into the hushed rhythm of waking streets.

The path to the park remained unchanged, yet with each passing day, it seemed to recognize them, folding them into its morning routine. The newspaper vendor barely looked up anymore—he already knew their names without knowing them. The stray dog at the tea stall stretched and yawned as if expecting them. And somewhere, in the rustling trees, the wind carried the faintest echo of laughter.

Their walks lasted exactly thirty minutes—not a minute more, not a minute less—as if someone had measured and decided it long ago. They never questioned this, simply following the rhythm each day, knowing precisely when it was time to move to the next part of their routine.

Fifteen minutes on the wooden bench. That was the rule. They sat, side by side, never questioning the ritual, letting the silence stretch between them as naturally as the sky turning from night to day.

And then, the day unfolded as it always did.

Breakfast. A brief pause. And then, the library.

Books had always been his retreat, a world that neither demanded nor questioned. Three hours, every day, spent in quiet companionship with words that never asked for anything in return.

She never cared for books.

Yet, there she was.

At first, just another presence in the morning air, a quiet shadow that lingered at a distance. But soon, her footsteps matched his, her voice slipping into the spaces between his thoughts.

The library was two kilometers away. The walk was long, but the words never ran out. Or rather, her words never ran out. She spoke of everything and nothing, her voice weaving through the dust-laden streets, filling the silence he had once carried so easily.

Inside, she would take a book from the shelf—never to read, only to hold. The pages remained unturned, her fingers resting lightly against the cover, as if waiting. Waiting for him to look up. Waiting for him to see.

He never did.

Or perhaps, he pretended not to.

The walk back was different. The books were issued, the conversations resumed, and the sugarcane vendor had already learned their order. She had grown fond of the taste—at first, because it was his choice, but soon, because it had become theirs.

Afternoons drifted in the same rhythm—lunch, quiet rest, and then, the evening.

Evening settled over the city in quiet hues, the warmth of the afternoon fading into a cooler, lingering breeze. The sky deepened, streaked with traces of retreating sunlight, and the park slowly filled with familiar sounds—the rustling of leaves, the rhythmic chatter of children, the occasional crack of a cricket bat meeting the ball.

He stepped onto the field, gripping the bat, feeling the weight of familiarity settle in his hands. The game had always been an escape, a space where thought was unnecessary, where movement replaced words. The earth beneath his feet felt steady, the boundary lines unchanged, and yet, something was different.

In the far corner of the park, she would be there.

She had no interest in cricket, yet she found herself on the same bench every evening, watching. Her friends sat beside her, their laughter blending with the evening air, but she barely heard them.

She watched.

At every shot, her fingers curled slightly, resisting the urge to clap. And when he smiled—just for a fleeting second—she found herself smiling too, though she never quite knew why.

Pranav noticed.

From the very first day, he noticed.

How she lingered in places where he happened to be. How her voice softened when she spoke to him. How, even in silence, she was always there.

Her presence was not an accident.

And yet, her presence did something else too.

It reached into places he had shut away, stirring memories he had spent years burying.

A familiar ache crept in, unwelcome and sudden.

The way she waited. The way she looked at him.

It was something he had seen before.

Something he had once lived through.

Something he had chosen to forget.

And yet, there it was again.

The weight of unspoken words. The quiet longing in someone's eyes. The silent presence of someone who stayed—even when he never asked them to.

Trapta's presence, her unwavering attachment, was pulling him into a past he had tried so hard to leave behind.

The past he had once run from.

But the past had a way of finding its way back.

And this time, it had returned—wrapped in the quiet, steady gaze of a girl who didn't know she had reopened an old wound.

He tried.

For days, he tried.

To change his routine. To carve a new path that wouldn't lead to her.

Morning walks were abandoned, replaced by the solitude of a quiet room. The library, once a ritual of companionship, became an isolated retreat in the afternoons. Even the playground, where he once sought freedom in cricket, was left untouched.

Yet, no matter how much he changed his steps, his thoughts refused to follow.

She lingered.

Not in presence, but in the spaces he had carved to forget her.

A week passed. And then, on an ordinary afternoon, as he walked back from the library, fate betrayed him once again.

"Hi, Pranav!"

Trapta's voice cut through the stillness, as if she had been waiting for this moment.

He turned, hesitating.

"Where have you been?" she asked, her brows knitting in concern.

"I... I just rescheduled my routine," he replied, his voice measured. "This way, I get more time to read books."

She fell silent, her gaze lingering on him longer than he was comfortable with.

"And while rescheduling, you didn't think of informing me?" she asked, her voice softer now, but edged with something he couldn't ignore.

He looked away.

"I thought you were unwell, Pranav. I didn't disturb you because I assumed you needed rest. But today, when I went to your house, I found out the truth."

He stiffened.

"You were trying to avoid me."

It wasn't a question. It was a quiet statement.

"But why?" she asked, her voice barely above a whisper. "I am really disappointed in you."

For the first time, he heard hurt in her voice. And something else—something that made his chest feel heavier than before.

Pranav had never been good at refusing people. His heart had always been too soft, his emotions too fragile to bear the weight of hurting another.

And now, sitting on the bench they had once claimed as their own, he found himself breaking his own resolve.

The wind carried the echoes of a past he had buried, pulling at the edges of memories he had sworn never to return to.

And with a heavy heart, he spoke.

CHAPTER 19

Trapta's presence lingered in the silence between them. She sat beside him, still, waiting. Unaware of the storm she had stirred—or perhaps knowing, but choosing not to press.

The evening air carried a strange stillness—the kind that lingers just before the first drop of rain touches dry earth. The park, once alive with scattered voices and laughter, now felt distant—not empty, but far away, as if belonging to another time.

He shifted slightly, his fingers curling around the edge of the bench, grounding himself. He exhaled, slow and deliberate, as if bracing for something unseen.

She said nothing.

And yet, her presence was enough.

It pulled at something buried deep, something long untouched but never forgotten.

And just like that, the lines between past and present blurred.

A familiar ache. A memory, sharp yet distant—like an old wound that had faded, but never fully healed.

The world around him softened. The rustling leaves, the hum of the city, the faint laughter—they were all still there, yet somehow slipping away.

The bench beneath him was no longer there.

The evening breeze stilled.

And suddenly, everything had changed—not just the moment, but the time itself.

April 2002 unfolded—a time when textbooks smelled new, when the weight of final exams still felt distant, and when the last year of school stretched ahead like an endless road, untouched by urgency.

And somewhere within that unfolding year, a boy sat in a quiet classroom, unaware of how the months ahead would shape him.

He was an average student—not brilliant enough to stand out, nor careless enough to be scolded. The kind teachers glanced over in roll call, whose presence they acknowledged but never truly noticed.

"Pranav, try to be more extroverted. Your shy nature may affect you professionally," his English teacher would often say, her voice laced with mild disapproval, as if shyness were a flaw that needed correcting.

He would nod—always nod—because that was easier than explaining that he didn't know how to be anything else.

Even though he had studied in a co-ed school all his life, he had never really had a female friend. Not since Class 6.

It wasn't that he had never tried. He had.

There were moments—small, fleeting ones—where he had spoken, where a conversation had almost begun. But they never lasted. Some invisible line, drawn long ago, remained firm.

Friendships had rearranged themselves, as if by an unseen force. Lunch tables, once open and shared, had restructured. Voices that once called his name easily, now spoke only in passing.

Somewhere along the way, he had become an acquaintance, never a friend.

Perhaps it was because he lacked the things that made people noticeable—money, attitude, and the kind of looks that made conversations effortless. He was neither loud nor striking. He didn't know how to take up space the way others did.

Or maybe, it was something simpler. Maybe he just wasn't interesting enough.

There were no harsh words, no deliberate exclusions—just a slow, quiet fading.

At some point, he had stopped trying. Not because he didn't want to, but because he no longer knew how.

Loneliness does not arrive suddenly. It grows, quietly, like a shadow that lengthens with time, until one day, it is all that remains.

And yet, he smiled.

Always smiled.

Because that was easier than asking why.

Because that was easier than admitting that somewhere, deep inside, it hurt.

And then, life unfolded in the most unexpected of ways.

The classroom carried its usual rhythm—the low hum of voices, the occasional thud of a book being dropped, the scraping of chairs against the uneven floor. The ceiling fan creaked as it spun, slicing the heavy summer air into reluctant swirls. Outside, the afternoon sun poured through the windows, casting lazy golden rectangles on the desks.

Somewhere near the window, in the third row from the back, a boy sat quietly. It was the best seat—not for its view of the blackboard, but for the quiet escape it offered.

Here, the world could be watched without being part of it. The gulmohar tree swayed gently in the afternoon breeze, its leaves catching the light. Beyond the school gate, bicycles rolled past, riders lost in their own destinations. Everything moved, effortlessly, while he remained still.

It was the kind of silence that had long settled in.

A silence that rarely broke.

No one usually disturbed him.

And then, something changed

The classroom hummed with its usual rhythm, but for the first time, something shifted in the air.

He sensed it before he saw it.

A presence. The faint shuffle of a chair being pulled back.

And before he could register it—she was there.

Not just anyone.

But Garima!

She wasn't just another student—she was the one everyone knew, the one who stood out without trying, the girl whose beauty and brilliance made her impossible to ignore.

Her hair, dark and glossy, framed her face perfectly, catching the light as she moved. Her eyes—deep, thoughtful—held a quiet intensity, as if they had seen more than others dared to.

There was something effortless about the way she carried herself, a kind of grace that made everyone around her stop and take notice. The boys, the teachers, even the walls seemed to lean in when she spoke, as if waiting to hear more.

She sat down beside him, and the space beside him, which had always been empty, felt filled with something—something heavier, something that shifted the very air between them.

For a brief moment, the classroom faded into the background. Her presence held the room in a way nothing else did.

As the days passed, she continued to sit beside him.

For the first time in months, he didn't mind. Her presence had become part of his routine, a quiet, unspoken thing that brought him a sense of comfort he hadn't known before.

It wasn't much, but it was enough.

And then, January 2003 came—quietly, without fanfare. The days moved slowly, the rhythm of school unchanged, yet somehow, he could feel something was different. The weight of the days before the exams started to settle, though the pressure had not yet arrived.

One day, in the midst of the usual classroom hum, something felt different.

It wasn't loud, it wasn't obvious, but the air felt heavier. His gaze shifted toward the door, then back to the desk in front of him.

For a moment, he wondered if things would remain the same after today. But he quickly pushed the thought aside. The space beside him felt like it always had—familiar, still his.

Then came that moment—when he overheard something he hadn't expected

CHAPTER 20

And then, just like that, the corridors fell silent. The walls stood in quiet patience, the classrooms no longer echoing with hurried footsteps. The classrooms, once filled with restless energy, now seemed to wait, knowing their oldest occupants were leaving—not forever, but for something bigger. Preparatory leave for the board exams had begun.

After today, she wouldn't be seen in these corridors again. The next meeting, if it happened at all, would be in another place, under different circumstances. The school, accustomed to her presence, would have to let go.

A pair of searching footsteps moved through the thinning crowd, pausing near familiar corners. The benches where she once sat, the spot outside the library where she often stood—each place was glanced at briefly, before moving on.

The walls listened, their echoes holding onto the last murmurs of departing students.

Near the canteen, a voice rose above the rest, and just like that, the steps slowed.

The steps halted. The canteen, once alive with voices and movement, seemed to close in around him. The walls, always indifferent to hurried conversations, stood still—as if listening too. Laughter floated past him, careless and light, but something beneath it felt heavier. The words were not meant for him, yet they reached him all the same.

Amidst the usual chatter, two voices stood out. A chair scraped against the floor, followed by the rustling of a paper wrapper. He didn't need to turn. He knew them. Garima's voice, familiar yet distant, carried the same ease it always had. And across from her, Prabal's, teasing, drawing laughter that felt lighter than it should have.

And just like that, something that had once felt whole, now quietly fell apart

The canteen had seen many conversations—some whispered, some loud, most forgotten within minutes. But this one, the walls seemed to hold onto. The air carried laughter, light and careless, drifting across the space like it had no weight.

"So, how are things going with Pranav, your love?" Prabal's voice slipped through the hum of conversations, casual and teasing, as he took a bite of his burger.

The walls, usually indifferent to such exchanges, seemed to pause. The wooden benches, scratched with years of restless hands, bore witness.

Laughter followed, effortless. "Pranav? My love? Oh, don't be silly, dear. I never loved him."

The ceiling fan turned lazily overhead, as if unconcerned. Prabal chuckled, shaking his head. "Oh, really? Then what's all that—gestures in class, all the eye talk?"

Garima's tone remained unchanged, light as ever. "Oh, come on, Prabal. Don't pull my leg. We both know I just used him—for Economics, nothing more."

The school had seen many names etched in gold—bright futures immortalized on the Hall of Fame Board. Garima wanted hers to be there, shining above the rest. But between her and that dream stood one subject—Economics.

She had always been clever, knowing whom to keep close. Prabal, a familiar name in both Pranav's world and hers, had suggested she take help from him. He knew Pranav well—too well. Emotional, sincere, the kind who would never refuse a friend in need. But even he hadn't expected her to play with emotions so easily.

Garima measured people the way she measured success—with precision. Handsome, wealthy, courageous. That was the standard. Prabal had all three. And so, when he asked again in Class 12, she had agreed.

The school had its own way of sorting people—those who stood out, and those who faded into the background. Garima had always known where she belonged. Her world was made of ambition, of names that deserved to be remembered. But not everyone fit into that world.

Pranav was different. He was decent-looking, but that alone wasn't enough. He lacked the ease, the presence, the effortless confidence that made heads turn. He didn't come from wealth, nor did he carry the kind of daring charm that made people listen. In the grand scheme of things, he was simply there. Reliable, unnoticed. The kind of person who was remembered only when needed.

For Garima, that was enough. For a while.

"But you have to tell him," Prabal's voice carried through the canteen, steady yet cautious. "As far as I know, he's started to develop feelings for you. When are you going to end it?"

Garima's response came without hesitation. "Soon. After the board exams. I'll be away for two months. After the results,

I'll move on, and that will be the end of it." Her tone was casual, unaffected, as if she were discussing the weather. "And since we won't bring it up, he'll never know."

Prabal exhaled, shaking his head. "Your plan…" he corrected, voice quieter now. "I was never part of it. I only suggested you seek his help because he was good at Economics. I never meant for you to play with his emotions." His voice dipped, as if debating whether to continue. "You should at least thank him."

Tell him the truth.

The words settled into the air, unnoticed by some, but not by the walls that had carried too many secrets. The fan turned overhead, indifferent to the weight in Prabal's voice. The canteen remained as it was—bustling, unconcerned, moving on. But not everything moved on. Some things stayed. Some things found a way to linger.

"You won't need to tell the truth, Prabal."

The words had nowhere to go. The walls, which had carried endless whispers before, now seemed to hold onto this one a little longer. The canteen, always indifferent to the stories it housed, settled into a brief silence, as if the air itself had paused. The fan turned above, unbothered by the weight that now lingered beneath it.

A voice rose—not loud, not accusing, just there.

He had heard enough. He wasn't one for crowds, nor for loud words. But that didn't mean he was blind. Or foolish. People thought quiet ones didn't notice. But they did. He did. And he had felt it too—the sting of being taken for granted.

No one interrupted. Garima's laughter had vanished, lost somewhere between surprise and amusement. Prabal shifted slightly, the crinkle of a paper wrapper the only sound between them.

The school had seen many departures, footsteps fading into corridors that had long learned to forget. But some moments refused to be forgotten. Some footsteps left echoes.

His steps were steady, unhurried, disappearing into the corridor. The canteen, after a pause, carried on—voices returning, chairs scraping, as if nothing had changed.

But the walls knew. And the walls never forgot.

CHAPTER 21

That was the last time a genuine smile touched his lips. And after that day, three things quietly slipped away—love, friendship, and above all, trust.

The memories receded quietly, leaving only a silent ache in their wake.

The park had not changed. The bench beneath him remained the same—steady, unmoved, waiting. Trapta's presence lingered quietly, patiently. The silence between them stretched, gentle yet heavy, waiting for words yet to be spoken.

Trapta sat beside him, quiet as ever. She had said nothing. Not then, not now. But something had shifted. The past, relentless in its return, had come and gone, leaving behind only silence.

The evening stretched on, unchanged. And yet, the moment that had just passed no longer belonged to it.

And he continued…

1st April 2003. The last board exam. A day of parting. And parting, after all, is always painful. The final chapter of a glorious book was coming to an end in just three hours. The golden period had passed—like a happy dream, vanishing before one could hold onto it.

The exam Centre carried a strange weight, filled with a concoction of emotions—sadness, relief, excitement, and something else. Something harder to name. Some wore broad smiles, their voices high with celebration, while others blinked away quiet tears as they handed their answer sheets to the invigilator.

They were free. And yet, they weren't.

Laughter, promises, hurried exchanges of landline numbers filled the air. Friends hugged, made plans, swore they'd stay in touch, already mapping out the next day. But something about it felt fragile—like words spoken against the wind, already fading before they could settle.

And then, he saw Garima.

For the last time.

The moment passed. The voices around him swelled again, full of plans, full of goodbyes. But he remained still. Some things end in words. Some, in silence.

And just like that, the story was over.

The words had settled, but they did not leave. Some words linger, hanging in the air long after they have been spoken.

"You should forget her," the voice was calm, steady. "You really loved her, but she did not love you back. She just used you to score well in the board exams."

The evening breeze stirred, carrying with it a weight that neither of them acknowledged.

She shifted slightly, rising to her feet. It was only then that they both noticed—her fingers had remained around his, firm and unmoving. A moment ago, they had spoken of parting, of loss, of things that could not be undone. And yet, here she was, holding on.

A quiet gaze met hers. Their eyes locked for a moment, as if searching for something unspoken.

"What?" she asked, breaking the silence.

"Nothing. Just reading your eyes."

A pause. A frown. "Reading my eyes?"

A nod. "I read somewhere that if you want to know the truth, look into someone's eyes. Eyes never lie."

She hesitated for a brief second. "And what did you see?" The voice was quieter now, less certain, more curious.

The answer did not come immediately. A hesitation, a breath, the search for the right words.

"Your eyes…" The words came slowly, as if searching for their place.

There was something about them—deep, quiet, yet holding an unspoken weight. A shade of brown that did not just reflect light but seemed to hold it, like earth after the first rain—rich, knowing, and undisturbed.

Eyes that did not demand attention, yet once noticed, were impossible to look away from. There was a certainty in them, not of arrogance, but of someone who had always known more than she let on.

For a moment, he wondered—had they always been this way? Had he simply never looked closely enough?

Another pause. A voice softer now. "And I am sorry."

A blink. "Sorry? For what?"

"Tomorrow at 5 a.m. For the walk. And then, the library."

She rolled her eyes dramatically, sighing loudly, "No! I hate the library!

The moment shifted, lightened. The weight between them did not vanish, but it softened—like a wound that had yet to heal, but no longer bled.

CHAPTER 22

The mornings unfolded as they always had—the same footsteps tracing the same path, the same silence resting between them like an old habit. Yet, something had changed. The past, which once loomed over him, had started to slip away—not because he had tried to forget, but because, somewhere along the way, forgetting had become effortless. And Trapta was always there—unhurried, unbothered, filling spaces he didn't know had been empty.

It hadn't taken her long to realize he was different. While others spoke without thinking, he thought without speaking. Where some searched for the right words, he seemed perfectly fine without them. There were boys who laughed too loudly, boys who competed to be noticed, boys who believed every silence was a problem to be solved. And then, there was him.

He was the sort of person who would listen to a joke, blink twice, and move on—not because he didn't understand it, but because he didn't know what was expected of him next. If happiness knocked, he would probably open the door, nod politely, and close it again without a word. If sadness arrived, it would have to wait in the corridor, unnoticed.

Yet, there was always a smile on his face. Not the kind that came from joy, but the kind that sat there because it had nowhere else to go. It was the same in every situation—a good day, a bad day, an ordinary day. A smile that fooled most people. But not her.

She had seen it more than once—on evenings when he spoke less than usual, on afternoons when his gaze drifted away mid-conversation, on mornings when he nodded instead of answering. But he never spoke about it. His troubles were like guests at a gathering—kept entertained somewhere in the background while he made sure everyone else was comfortable.

And somewhere between his unreadable expressions and her quiet observations, she had begun to fall.

There was a simplicity in him—not the kind that lacked depth, but the kind that made everything else seem unnecessary. An honesty that wasn't spoken, but felt.

He never said much—not in words, not in grand gestures. But she saw it. In the way he always walked slightly behind in a group, letting others lead. In the way he never interrupted, even when he had something to say. In the way his presence never demanded attention, yet never felt missing.

He would never say it first. She knew that.

But in his silences, she had found her answer.

And just like that, without knowing when it started, he had begun to notice her more than before.

It was the little things that began to stand out—the way her smile seemed to linger even after she had turned away, the sound of her voice that seemed to follow him even when she wasn't speaking. The way she walked, not with any hurry, as though the day would unfold on its own time, and the way her eyes would catch his, not demanding anything, just acknowledging something unspoken between them. He hadn't noticed when it started, but somehow, it had become impossible to ignore.

Her presence, though quiet, was everywhere—like a thread woven into the fabric of his days, pulling him in a direction he hadn't anticipated.

And just like that, before he could understand it, the result day arrived.

The result had been waiting. It had always been there, silent and certain, watching from a distance, knowing its moment would come. It wasn't impatient—it preferred to let the anticipation build, stretching time longer than it should.

But he had a plan. A foolproof plan. Sleep late, wake up just in time, and check the result when the dust had settled, when the world had already reacted. No endless waiting, no unnecessary suffering.

But the result had its own ideas.

It nudged him awake far too early, long before he wanted to open his eyes. He turned in bed, pulled the blanket over his head, convinced that if he ignored it, it might disappear. But the result was persistent. It sat there, heavy and unmoving, stretching the minutes, making sure he couldn't forget.

When the time arrived, he sat in front of the computer, fingers hovering over the keyboard, his mother standing silently behind him. The result could feel his hesitation, but it wasn't going to make things easy.

The page began to load. And load. The result enjoyed the suspense. It pretended to appear, then vanished. It teased, lingering just out of reach.

Two hours passed.

The progress bar crawled forward, moving at its own pace—like a tired clerk flipping through dusty files. The spinning wheel twirled lazily, taunting him. The result was in no hurry. Across the city, parents had started logging in at midnight, as if shaking the website awake would make it respond faster.

(Back then, in 2003, the internet was in no hurry either. Pages loaded at their own pace, testing patience in ways no exam ever could.)

And then, without announcement or drama, the result revealed itself—calm, indifferent, as though it had always known this moment would come.

The next morning, they met as usual. The tension of the previous day had faded, leaving behind only quiet acceptance.

CHAPTER 23

Life had shifted—not suddenly, not loudly, but in the quiet way that time moves forward, unnoticed.

The mornings were no longer the same. The old paths still existed, but they led elsewhere now. His bag, once carrying nothing but books, now carried a cricket kit, a register, a pair of socks, and fresh clothes—his routine, neatly packed between them.

At dawn, he was already on the field. The bat met the ball, the air carried the sharp sound of practice, and exhaustion settled into his bones long before the city had woken up. A quick bath, breakfast at the club canteen, and then the rush to catch the bus to college.

The afternoons passed in a blur—lectures, assignments, numbers on a blackboard. But before the day could even slow down, he was back on the field again, gripping the bat tighter, training harder. The sun dipped, the drills continued, and by the time he returned home, sleep found him before he could think of anything else.

Somewhere else, another routine had formed.

She left for college later, when the roads were already filled with people. The library she passed every day was the same, but the bench where they had once sat together, where time had once paused for them, remained untouched. The playground she passed in the evening was louder than before, but the game felt different. She had never played, never even pretended to care for the game, but still, she had watched.

Now, she kept walking.

She never complained. She knew his dream, and she would never ask him to meet her instead. But sometimes, without realizing it, her steps slowed near the ground. Her gaze lingered for just a moment longer than it should have, before she reminded herself that he was not there—not as before, not in the way she had once been used to.

They waited for Sunday.

At dawn, they met. The path was the same, the air familiar, the pauses between conversations as effortless as before. Neither of them spoke about the days in between, nor did they need to. And then, just as the morning softened, he was gone—to the ground, to the bat, to the dream that had been calling him long before she ever had.

She returned home, counting the hours until the next Sunday would come.

The days slipped into months, and the months stretched into years. Time moved forward, unnoticed, yet their world remained untouched. The routine never wavered—morning walks, shared laughter, and the quiet certainty that Sundays belonged to them.

And now, without realizing when, the final year of college had arrived. The walks were the same, the words effortless, the teasing familiar. Yet, something had changed. Not in the routine, not in the silences, but in the way his gaze lingered a moment longer, in the way she hesitated before saying goodbye.

Love had settled in—not as a sudden realization, but as something that had always been there, growing quietly between them, waiting to be understood.

Three years had quietly passed, and yet, their Sundays remained unchanged—routine, comfortable, but with something deeper growing between them, almost unnoticed.

They met one Sunday evening.

The evening deepened, stretching its quiet arms across the sky. The last traces of daylight lingered stubbornly on the horizon, fading slowly as night tiptoed in. The soft hum of the world winding down surrounded them—distant footsteps, an occasional bicycle bell, the rustling of leaves dancing in the evening breeze.

Above them, the moon had begun to rise, round and full, casting silver light over the park. It was the kind of night that seemed to pause time, where even the shadows looked softer, the air felt gentler, and silence carried more meaning than words.

The street lamps flickered on, one by one, their golden glow blending with the moonlight. Somewhere in the distance, a lone cricket chirped—a quiet reminder of the nights they had never shared before.

The world was settling, but something about this night felt like it had just begun.

They walked side by side, their footsteps in perfect rhythm, but there was a difference—a quiet one that neither spoke of. The laughter, the teasing, the little nudges—they were all there, but they felt like echoes of something that once was, like the air around them had become heavier with everything they hadn't said.

They reached the bench—the same one they had shared countless mornings, the one where their silences had never felt awkward, where words had once flowed and sometimes never came at all.

They sat down, not rushing, not speaking. The night didn't demand words, and for the first time, neither did they.

But everything about this evening was different.

He was no longer the boy who spent his days chasing a dream on the field, swinging a bat under the scorching sun. Cricket had become a memory, one he had let go of in the pursuit of something else, something more concrete. His days were now consumed with books, numbers, thoughts of an MBA, and what came next. The weight of exams, final projects, and an uncertain future pressed on him more than ever. And yet, tonight, all of that felt distant.

And right now, none of it mattered.

She turned toward him, her eyes searching—seeking something he wasn't sure he had the words for. He didn't need to say anything. He could feel the question in the air between them, thick with everything they had been through and everything that still lingered unspoken.

And then, before he could understand it, she leaned in. Her arms gently reached around him, pulling him closer, just enough for her to feel the quiet strength of him—steady, unshaken, but somehow softer than before.

He did not move.

Not stiff, not uncertain—just still. He didn't reject her, but neither did he embrace her. It was as though the moment demanded something more than just action. It was as though their silence had been enough for both of them.

Her warmth, the quiet rise and fall of her breath against him, felt like the slow unfolding of everything they had quietly known but never allowed to come forward. The heartbeat she felt against her cheek was steady, unsure, yet unguarded.

She closed her eyes, feeling his presence, listening to the rhythm of something unspoken, something they had always felt but never said.

Then, in a voice softer than the night itself, she whispered into his ear:

"I'll be yours for all the births we take in this world."

And in that moment, everything around them faded away. The world, the noise, the years ahead—none of it existed anymore. There was only this moment, only the two of them, together in their own world.

They were in their own universe, untouched by time.

CHAPTER 24

The bench had never spoken a word in its lifetime, yet it had known more stories than the wind that rustled through the park. It had listened to whispers of old men reminiscing their youth, felt the restless energy of children climbing its wooden arms, and held the weight of tired laborers who needed nothing but a moment's rest.

But they—they had been different.

They hadn't just sat.

They had made the bench their own.

Their voices had seeped into its wooden slats, their laughter had settled into its frame, their silence had stretched across its surface like an invisible thread holding them together.

The bench had been there from the very first day—when one had watched and the other had run.

It had been there when they had walked side by side, unspoken words filling the space between their footsteps. It had felt the warmth of their conversations, the weight of their dreams, the moments when their laughter had been so effortless that the evening air had carried it beyond the trees.

It had also been there when the laughter had faded.

When words had turned into quiet sighs.

When long pauses had replaced easy conversations.

It had wanted to interfere once. Especially the day they had argued—her voice sharp, his quieter but firm. For the first time, the bench had wished it had arms, just so it could nudge them closer. But, like all good listeners, it had stayed silent, knowing some stories needed their own space to unfold.

And then there had been the nights.

Not just one.

Not just two.

But many.

The kind where the moon had watched over them, where the air had been thick with something unspoken, where she had leaned against him, and he had not moved.

It had felt the moment she had wrapped her arms around him.

It had felt the moment he had not held her back—but had not pulled away either.

It had felt the moment her voice had softened, almost trembling, as she whispered into his ear.

And just like that, they had become a part of it.

The bench had missed them when they stopped coming every day.

But it had not been sad.

It had understood. There were seasons for everything. Even love. Even friendship. Even silence.

And if they were not there, it meant they were chasing something bigger.

And so, it had waited.

It had made sure it was empty each morning, untouched each evening, saving their place the way a friend saves a seat.

It had believed.

But today—something was different.

The morning air was cool, the park untouched by the rush of the city.

Everything was the same—the wind played with the leaves, the morning walkers moved along the familiar paths, the birds chattered as always.

But he was different.

The bench felt it the moment he sat down.

He did not sit in his usual way—not with the quiet ease of someone who belonged there. His shoulders carried a weight the bench had never felt before. His hands rested on his lap, but not in relaxation.

He had sat with the heaviness of someone who had already braced for impact, already prepared for the words that were to come....

And then the bench saw it.

A small piece of folded paper, clutched between his fingers.

Not just any paper.

A note.

The one she had given him last night.

And whatever had happened last night had changed everything.

The night had welcomed them as it always did.

The air was thick with the scent of damp earth, the cool breeze humming softly through the trees, carrying whispers of old conversations. The moon, half-hidden behind drifting clouds, cast silver patterns on the grass. Even the leaves, scattered in uneven patches across the ground, seemed to pause, as if making space for them—just as they had always done.

And the bench—though it never spoke—had known they would come.

They settled in, familiar and unhurried. She sat first, her fingers brushing the wood absentmindedly. He followed, quieter than usual, but the silence between them did not feel out of place. Not yet.

For a while, it felt like every other night.

Until it wasn't.

Because tonight, as their voices wove through the stillness, the bench heard a name it had never heard before.

Rohan

Her lips parted, and the past slipped through them. Not rushed, not hesitant—just steady, carrying a weight the bench had never felt before. Her voice, once light as the evening air, now moved through the stillness like a quiet confession, pulling memories into the open, one word at a time.

Her voice did not waver, yet something in it was unsteady— as if it had been holding back a tide that could no longer be contained. The words came not as a revelation, but as something already known, something that had always existed, just never spoken aloud. And now, they drifted into the night, settling into the silence like fallen leaves on water—weightless, yet impossible to ignore.

His name did not just belong to the night—it belonged to the years before it. And as she spoke, her voice did not simply carry words; it carried time itself, folding back the pages of a story that had begun long before this evening.

Rohan had always been there. Since the second grade, through half-erased pencil marks on notebooks and hurried bites of lunchboxes shared between classes, through whispered answers during dictation tests and noisy bus rides home. Their names had always been called together—on attendance registers, on group assignments, in the casual roll call of teachers who no longer needed to check the list.

By the time they reached tenth grade, love was not something they found—it was something that had always been waiting for them. It did not arrive suddenly, nor did it ask for permission. It was in the way he carried her books when her hands were full, in the way she saved the last bite of her chocolate for him, in the way their laughter felt different when they were together.

And in twelfth grade, when the world around them spoke of college admissions and uncertain futures, they had made a promise—not in grand declarations or borrowed lines from movies, but in the quiet certainty of two people who had already chosen each other.

Then, like all stories that stretch beyond school corridors, life moved forward. Rohan had to leave—not in heartbreak, not in reluctance, but in the way the next page of a book must always be turned. He had promised to come back, and she had believed him. She had watched him walk away, not as someone leaving, but as someone who would return.

And for a while, she had waited. Until one morning, when she had seen someone else—someone who did not belong to her past, someone who did not carry shared childhood memories, someone who had simply been there, in a park, running away from a voice he had not expected to hear.

Her voice carried forward, but it was no longer just recounting memories—it was unraveling something deeper, something she had kept hidden even from herself. The words slipped out, quiet at first, then stronger—like a tide that had been waiting too long to rise.

She had not planned it this way.

She had not meant for it to happen.

And yet, it had.

It had begun the moment she first saw him in the park. The one who had turned at the sound of her voice only to run. The one who had tried to remain unseen, but whom she could not unsee after that day.

Rohan had left with a promise, but promises do not fill empty spaces. Loneliness is clever—it does not announce itself; it lingers, stretching the days, making the silence louder. And that day, when she saw him sitting there, quiet, hesitant, withdrawn from the world in a way she understood too well—her mind had spoken before her heart had a chance.

Talk to him.

He will make this easier.

He will fill the silence.

And she had listened.

Her heart had whispered warnings in between—the kind of warnings that come too late. There had been moments when she had almost told him. When his words had carried too much honesty, too much trust. When he had spoken about Garima, when he had told her of the ache that still lived within him. Her heart had stirred then, pushed against the weight of her silence, begged her to speak.

But her mind had won.

Don't. If you tell him, you will lose this too.

So, she had stayed.

Not because he was what she had wanted, but because he had been there. Because he had been steady, unshaken in his ways. Because in his silence, she had found an escape from her own. Because when he listened, he listened completely, without questioning, without demanding more than she could give.

She had believed it was harmless.

But she had known the truth long before tonight.

And then, Rohan had returned.

Tonight, should have been different. Tonight, should have been about happiness. But all she had felt was the weight of everything left unsaid. The words had unraveled from her before she could stop them. And now, they hung in the air between them, unchangeable.

She had told him everything.

And for the first time since she had met him, he had said nothing.

No anger. No outburst. No accusations.

Just silence.

The same silence that had once felt comforting now pressed against her like something unbearable.

She reached into her bag, her fingers brushing against the small folded note she had carried with her all evening. She had written it hours ago, before she had even known if she would give it to him.

But now, as she looked at him, she knew she had no choice.

Her hand trembled as she placed it beside him on the bench.

A final offering. A final apology.

She hesitated, just for a second. Long enough to wonder if she should take it back. But then, she turned.

And she left.

The wind rustled through the trees, lifting the note slightly before letting it settle again.

The bench, which had held their laughter, their quiet conversations, their silences—felt the weight of something else now.

And the night, which had always welcomed them, watched as one remained seated, and the other disappeared into the darkness

But the night did not let go so easily.

The silence stretched, thick and unmoving, settling into the spaces where words had once been.

The trees swayed, the wind whispered, but the bench remained still, watching as he, too, finally rose and walked away—his footsteps slower than they had ever been.

CHAPTER 25

The night had settled in, wrapping the world in its quiet stillness. Inside, Trapta sat on the edge of her bed, hands clasped together, eyes fixed on the telephone. It had been a long time since she had felt this unsure. The room carried the stillness of a space waiting for a decision to be made. Her mind had already drawn its conclusions—clear, sharp, unwavering. "You did the right thing. You told him everything. Now walk away." But her heart, though weaker, was persistent. "He will come."

She shook her head, trying to silence the voice that had begun to stir deep within her. The mind was quick to counter. "And what will that change? The past? Your choices? Nothing."

The argument had begun the moment she had left him at the bench, and now, sitting here, staring at the telephone as if it held an answer, she found herself at war with the very instincts that had guided her all this time.

She had watched him just moments ago, the way his fingers had curled around the note, the way he had remained silent even when she had expected anger, accusations—anything but the unbearable quiet he had given her. That silence should have been enough. It should have been the end.

But something about it lingered.

Her heart whispered again, softer this time. "But he will come."

She inhaled sharply. For months, she had listened to her mind—choosing what was easier over what was right. But tonight, as she sat amidst the silence, the mind did not feel right. Without allowing herself to think any further, she reached for the receiver. The rings stretched into the distance. One. Two. Three. A soft click. She didn't wait. Didn't give herself time to reconsider.

"Tomorrow morning. Same place."

That was all she said before placing the receiver back. The phone settled into its cradle with a finality that made her close her eyes. She had not listened to her mind tonight.

The night faded, but it did not take everything with it.

The morning air had carried the scent of damp leaves, the kind that lingers after a night of unsettled winds. The bench had felt the weight of him before, but today, it was different. There was no pause, no moment of stillness before settling in.

He had sat with the heaviness of someone who had already braced for impact, already prepared for the words that were to come....

The note still rested in his hands, creased at the edges, its silence heavier than its words.

And then, a presence beside him.

There had been no hesitation, no uncertain pause before sitting down. The bench knew the warmth well, the familiar weight that had once leaned against it with quiet trust. But today, that warmth carried something different. A tremor, perhaps. An unease woven into the very air between them.

A breath, slow and measured. And then, finally, words. Soft, deliberate, yet carrying the weight of everything left unsaid for too long.

"I am sorry. Please forgive me."

The wind shifted slightly, rustling the leaves, as if the park itself had paused to listen.

"I never wanted to hurt you."

The bench had heard many words before—laughter spilling carelessly into the open, quiet conversations that did not need to be finished, promises made in whispers under moonlit skies. But these words were different. They did not carry the certainty of the past. They carried an ending.

"I cannot forget you."

For a moment, the bench almost believed it.

"But I cannot live without him."

The stillness deepened.

The note between his fingers crumpled slightly, not by force, but by the slow, unconscious movement of someone absorbing each word, one by one, letting them settle like dust on an untouched surface.

She was waiting—for what, the bench did not know. A reaction, perhaps. A word. A sigh. Anything to break the silence that now stretched between them.

But he did not speak.

And in that silence, she lowered her gaze, as if realizing that the forgiveness she sought would not be spoken aloud.

For a long while, he said nothing. The note still rested in his hands; its edges slightly curled from the pressure of his fingers. The ink had not faded, yet something about the words felt distant now—like a promise too late, an apology that could no longer be undone.

And then, finally, a breath. A shift in the way his shoulders carried their weight.

When he spoke, his voice was quieter than it had ever been, yet it cut through the silence like something sharp.

"You are a great actor."

She inhaled sharply.

His gaze did not meet hers. He did not accuse, did not demand an explanation. He simply stated it—like a fact, like something undeniable.

"You were able to lie with your eyes."

She flinched.

The wind stirred between them, lifting a stray leaf before settling again. Her fingers curled against her lap, tightening, as if holding onto something that was no longer there.

A tear slipped down her cheek before she could stop it.

And then—warmth.

Not in words, not in comfort, but in the quietest of gestures.

His fingers, rough with the weight of unspoken things, reached out and wiped the tear away. It should not have meant anything. It should not have made her want to cry more.

But it did.

His touch lingered only for a moment before he pulled back. And when he spoke again, there was no anger. Just something heavier.

"I was upset with you when you told me about Rohan."

The name hung between them like an unfinished sentence.

"I never thought I'd have to talk about any of this with you. I never wanted to. But… it hurt." His fingers tightened around the note. "I always considered you a great friend. And maybe that was my mistake."

The words pressed into the space between them, into the cracks neither had acknowledged.

"You knew," he continued, his voice steady, almost too steady. "You knew what I felt. And you let it be. You let me believe in something that never existed."

She could not meet his eyes.

"If you had told me earlier," he said, exhaling, "I would have understood. I would have tried to be your friend." His voice dropped lower, heavier. "But you didn't. And that… that is what hurts more than anything."

The weight of the confession settled over them, thick and inescapable.

"You hurt me more than Garima ever did."

She shut her eyes.

A slow breath.

A pause long enough to feel unbearable.

And then—

"But since you've realized your mistake, I have completely forgiven you."

Her eyes snapped open.

The words should have felt like relief. They should have lifted the weight pressing on her chest.

But they didn't.

They were not spoken with resentment. Nor with warmth.

They were simply final.

His fingers unfolded the note once more, staring at it for a second longer before finally letting it rest on the bench beside him.

A quiet sigh.

"All the best for your new life," he said.

She swallowed. Nodded. It was all she could do.

For the first time, she felt like the one who had been left behind.

"I… I still have your landline number," she said, her voice uneven. "I'll call you."

A pause.

A flicker of something unreadable in his eyes.

"I am relocating soon," he said finally.

It was the first thing he had said that surprised her.

She parted her lips, but no words came.

The wind stirred again, lifting the note slightly before letting it settle once more.

"Do call me if you want to," she said. "And give me your number." Her voice was quieter now. "I'll be here for a few more years."

A silence stretched between them.

And then, just as softly, almost as if he hadn't meant for her to hear—

"I will try."

It was the last thing he said.

And then, without hesitation, he rose.

The morning stretched, the sun rising a little higher, casting long shadows where they had once sat.

The bench had held them for so long. Their conversations, their silences, their laughter, their heartbreaks—it had absorbed everything, made space for all of it. And now, it held only their memory. A memory that, with time, would soften, blur, and fade into the quiet hum of the world moving forward.

And soon, even that would drift into the passing breeze.

But the bench was not the only one watching.

The park had been waiting for him long before he ever knew it. It had welcomed him on that first morning, when his hesitant steps had carried the weight of someone searching for something unknown. It had held the echoes of his footprints, had listened to his thoughts as he walked its paths, had watched as he ran—away from a voice, toward something he did not yet understand.

And today, the park knew.

It knew this was the end.

The wind stirred, lifting the leaves in slow, sweeping circles, as if trying to hold onto him for just a little longer. The trees, which had once swayed to his quiet presence, now stood still, their branches reaching toward the sky, as if in farewell. The morning air, once so crisp and welcoming, felt heavier, knowing it would never hold his presence the same way again.

He walked—not hurried, not hesitant, just... final.

He did not turn back.

The park did not call out to him. It had known him well enough to understand—he would not return.

The path stretched ahead, winding toward an exit he had passed through a hundred times before. But today, it was different. Today, he was not leaving with the promise of coming back.

And as the last trace of his shadow slipped beyond the gate, the park exhaled.

It had welcomed him once.

Now, it let him go.

A soft gust of wind whispered through the trees, brushing against the empty bench, before fading into the morning.

And just like that—he was gone

CHAPTER 26

The night stood still.

The house, usually humming with familiar sounds—the distant murmur of conversations, the rhythmic tick of the clock, the occasional clang of utensils in the kitchen—was wrapped in an unfamiliar silence. There was no one home. His parents and brother had left for a family visit, leaving behind only empty rooms and echoes of a presence that was no longer there.

The absence of sound should have been a comfort. But tonight, it was anything but.

The kitchen light cast a soft glow, stretching long shadows against the tiled floor. The air carried the faint aroma of cardamom, blending with the warmth of freshly boiled milk. He stood by the counter, stirring the Bournvita in slow, deliberate circles. The spoon clinked against the sides of the cup, the only sound breaking the weight of the stillness.

His movements were mechanical—pour, stir, watch the color change—actions repeated so often they required no thought. And yet, his mind was nowhere in the present. It lingered elsewhere, pulled back by something stronger than habit.

In his pocket, a folded piece of paper lay untouched.

It hadn't been there long, but it already weighed on him. Neatly placed, yet impossible to ignore. It hadn't moved, hadn't changed, and yet, it had occupied his thoughts every waking second.

A deep breath.

His fingers hesitated for a moment before reaching into his pocket and drawing it out, unfolding it carefully, as if it might crumble under the weight of the emotions trapped within its creases.

The words stared back at him.

Hope you will forgive me. I really didn't want to hurt you. I am extremely sorry. -Trapta

They were simple. Few in number, but heavy in meaning.

He read them once.

Then again.

The ink had not faded overnight, and yet, he still searched the page—as if hoping the words had changed.

But they hadn't.

A breath shuddered through him, uneven, laced with something unspoken. His fingers curled around the edges of the note, gripping it tighter, as if holding onto it might lessen the ache settling deep within his chest.

A single tear slipped down, landing softly on the paper.

He had known loss before. He had let people go before. So why did this feel different?

His eyes burned, but he did not wipe them. The note blurred for a second before his vision cleared, forcing him to read the words once more.

He exhaled sharply.

Why?

Why was he so emotionally attached to someone who was never his?

Why did it still hurt?

The spoon in his cup moved again, stirring the Bournvita in slow, measured circles. The liquid swirled, mirroring the thoughts inside him, each movement dragging him deeper—pulling him back, beyond the ache, beyond the questions, beyond the trembling note still in his hands.

And just like that, the past faded.

A soft glow illuminated his face.

The faint buzz of the Nokia 2280 screen cast a weak light against his palm. The phone, old yet familiar, had seen everything—every unread message, every unsent draft, every hesitation, every moment spent staring at a blank screen, waiting for words that never arrived.

Tonight, it was waiting again.

His fingers hovered over the keypad, unmoving at first. And then, with quiet determination, they began to type.

I've spent months trying to put this into words, but the truth is simple—I want you in my life, not just as a friend, but as someone I can share every moment with. Will you be mine?

The words blinked back at him.

He read them once.

Then again.

His left hand steadied the phone, his thumb hesitating over the send button. His right hand stirred the Bournvita, the spoon clinking softly against the cup—a rhythm too familiar, a memory too persistent.

For the first time in months, clarity cut through the fog of emotions. Aparna was not Trapta.

She had mentioned Girish. She had spoken of friendships and bonds. But she was honest.

Even if her answer was no, it would be honest.

He could live with that.

But what if… she had been waiting?

What if she had been waiting for him to say it first?

A deep breath.

A decision.

His thumb pressed the button.

A quiet beep followed.

The message had been sent.

Finally, the Nokia 2280 lay still.

Exhausted after carrying the weight of so many unsent words, it rested on the wooden table, its tiny screen flickering weakly in the dim light. For months, it had been a silent witness to hesitation—a message typed and erased, a name searched and abandoned. Tonight, however, it had fulfilled its purpose. The message had been sent.

For the first time in a long while, there was nothing more to do.

It did not know what had changed. Why its owner, after so many restless nights, had finally mustered the courage to press that button. It did not concern itself with reasons. Its duty was simple—to send and to receive. And yet, as it sat there, waiting in the hush of the night, even the Nokia 2280 could sense that something had shifted.

It had been through this routine before—an unread message blinking on the screen, an unsent draft held in limbo, a quiet sigh before the backlight dimmed into silence. But tonight was different. The message was not erased. The screen had not gone blank with hesitation.

Now, all that remained was the wait.

The phone's screen glowed feebly, illuminating the wooden table in a faint halo. Its battery was strong, its network signal steady. It was ready. But was the reply ready?

Minutes passed. The Nokia 2280, ever patient, sat unmoving.

Its owner, however, was far from still.

A hand reached out. Fingers tapped the plastic buttons, checking for a response that had not yet arrived. The phone, knowing its role well, obeyed—flashing the same screen, the same menu, the same absence of new messages. Nothing had changed. Not yet.

It was used to this. The waiting. The hoping. The silence.

At times, it wondered if humans ever understood their own hearts. They spent hours crafting messages, only to delete them. They held onto words they longed to say, letting them decay in drafts. And when they finally found the courage to speak, they were plagued by a new kind of fear—the fear of the reply.

The phone did not have such worries. It had sent the message. It had done its part.

Now, it was up to her.

Another check. Still no response.

The phone sighed—not aloud, of course. It was a sturdy device, not one of the newer, delicate models that whined for attention at the slightest command. It would not vibrate needlessly, nor blink without cause. It would wait.

And so, the Nokia 2280 remained as it was—still, silent, and patient.

Waiting, just as he was

And so, the wait began.

A press. A flicker. A pause. A sigh.

The same routine played out over and over again. The buttons were pressed with increasing impatience, the screen stared at as if sheer willpower could summon a response.

Nothing.

Then, an idea seemed to strike its owner.

The phone felt itself being turned over, inspected, as if something new might be discovered after all these years. It endured the scrutiny patiently.

Could it, perhaps, connect to her Nokia 1100?

A hidden frequency? A forgotten feature buried in the depths of old manuals?

The phone, if it had the ability, would have sighed. It had spent its life sending and receiving messages—it was not a telepathic device.

And yet, here it was, being tilted at different angles, held up toward the ceiling, as if catching an invisible signal might bridge the impossible distance.

It refused to cooperate.

The screen remained the same, unimpressed by such experiments.

A sigh from its owner. A defeated grip loosening.

The phone was placed back on the table.

Waiting.

The hesitation began to creep in, slow but steady.

A press. A flicker. The same screen, the same empty inbox.

His fingers moved on their own, scrolling through old messages. Reading. Rereading. Searching for reassurance in words that had not changed.

A name lingered longer than the others. Girish.

There it was—the message that had started it all. Was that why she hadn't replied? Had he lost another friend?

The fingers hesitated, then moved toward the call button.

One press.

A deep breath.

Cancelled.

A restless tap against the side of the phone. The screen dimmed again, its glow fading into silence.

Another attempt. Another hesitation.

A brief moment of bravery—the call screen appeared once again.

A pause. The numbers blinked back, waiting.

But hesitation was stronger.

The button was pressed.

Then released.

Nothing.

The phone, having witnessed this cycle one too many times, would have rolled its eyes—if only it had them.

The wait had stretched long enough for hope to settle into uncertainty.

Then, a vibration.

A soft beep, breaking through the stillness.

For a second, he didn't move. The phone, exhausted from its silent vigil, finally had something to show.

The screen flickered.

New Message from: Aparna

The breath caught in his throat. The fingers that had hesitated a hundred times before now trembled as they pressed the button.

The message opened.

Hello Manu... How are you?? Hope you are fine... Today 8PM will call you, be free.

The wait wasn't over.

It had delivered the message, received a reply, and now, it prepared itself for the next task. Something bigger. Something more uncertain.

The hours stretched, moving slower than usual. The phone could sense it—its owner checking it too often, flipping it open, staring at the screen before shutting it again. It was as if time itself had decided to take the scenic route.

A small vibration from a random network message.

The screen lit up.

The fingers moved instantly—quick, expectant.

Then, a pause.

A sigh.

The phone dimmed again.

It waited.

Any moment now.

The air around it felt heavier, like something was about to happen. It was used to waiting, but this time, there was something different. It had never carried a message quite like the one it sent a few days ago. It had never waited for a response quite like this.

And yet, the stillness continued.

The grip on its sides tightened for a moment. Then loosened. The fingers hesitated over the keypad, pressing nothing, scrolling through nothing.

A press. A flicker. A pause.

Nothing.

Had she forgotten?

It considered this thought for the first time. Had all that waiting been for nothing?

Another press. The same screen. The same emptiness.

It braced itself for disappointment.

Then—

A sudden vibration. A flicker of light. A sharp, distinct tone breaking through the silence.

It had heard many sounds before, but this was different.

A call.

The long wait had ended.

Now, something else was about to begin.

A faint signal flickered, and the long-awaited connection finally established itself.

"Took your time, didn't you?" Nokia 2280 grumbled, barely able to contain its frustration.

"Ah, you're awake!" Nokia 1100's voice crackled through, sounding far too relaxed. "I thought you'd exhausted yourself from all that unnecessary overthinking."

"Overthinking?!" 2280 nearly sputtered. "I've been sitting in silence for days! Do you have any idea how long I've waited? My circuits have aged a decade! If I had a heartbeat, I would've collapsed twice by now!"

"Dramatic as ever," 1100 sighed. "You really thought she wouldn't call? Tsk tsk… poor thing. So much stress for nothing."

2280 huffed. "Four days of silence is no joke! The waiting… the hesitation… the constant checking for messages that never arrived—it gets to you!"

1100 chuckled. "And yet, here we are. Just as I expected. He waited, you waited, and now, finally, she's here."

2280 hesitated. "Yes, but what took her so long?"

"Oh, wouldn't you like to know?" 1100's tone was teasing, almost smug. "Let's just say—she had her own reasons."

2280 flickered, feeling the faint vibrations of the moment arriving. The time had come. The air around it felt different now, heavier, expectant.

"Here we go," 1100 muttered.

The call had begun.

The voice on the other end did not hurry. It came gently, like someone stepping into a quiet room, aware that even the slightest sound could shift something fragile. For a few moments, there was only the faint hum of the line—steady, unbroken. It was she who spoke first, her words careful, as though selecting them from a shelf where emotions had been kept untouched for too long.

"Manu…" she said at last, her voice steady, but not without effort. "I read your message. I don't know what made you send it, especially after everything I told you. I had said it clearly… why complicate relations? Still, you sent it."

The words hung in the air, not sharp, but heavy—like something she had carried quietly for days and was now placing, gently, between them.

"I told you about Girish. Still, you chose to send that message…"

The name, once spoken, settled into the silence that followed. He didn't flinch, but something in the way his fingers held the phone gave him away.

"I thought over it," she said, and this time her voice was quieter. "See, Manu… we both have our careers ahead of us. You have to complete your CA, and I have to finish my probation. After that,

I'll get my first posting. Marriage is not something I can think about right now. I'm not ready. And you aren't either."

She didn't speak immediately after that. A pause lingered, soft and thoughtful. When she continued, her tone had changed—not by much, but just enough to be noticed.

"You finish your CA. Let me complete my first posting. And then… maybe after two years… I'll talk to my parents. They won't say no. They've known your family since childhood. They won't say no."

She didn't rush the next line. But there was something different now—gentler, almost amused.

"And then," she added, "we'll definitely get married.

He didn't respond immediately. A faint rustle on the other end suggested he had shifted in his seat. The phone, still pressed close to his ear, caught the sound of his breath—a little unsteady, almost as if he had forgotten how to breathe normally. His fingers, which had been motionless all this while, now moved slightly, tracing the edge of the phone in slow, unsure circles.

He was still holding onto her last words, trying to make sense of them without rushing. The silence on his end wasn't deliberate—it was the kind that comes when the heart understands something a little slower than the mind. A beat passed. Then, in a voice almost too casual for the moment, he asked, "So… does this mean you've declined my proposal?" The question wasn't sharp—only uncertain, as if he were still piecing her words together like a puzzle that almost fit but not quite.

For a second, even the phone seemed to sigh. After everything it had witnessed—drafts, hesitations, late-night pauses—it was almost absurd how slow he still was. If it had a voice, it might have muttered, "Bhai, ab toh samajh ja."

"Aree buddhu… itna bhi nahi samjhe?" her voice followed, half-laughing, half-scolding. It danced across the line, light and full of mischief. "I mean—I'll talk to my parents, they'll talk to yours, and then we'll get married. Happy now, you idiot?

Somewhere between the silence of the call and the fading tension, a quiet chuckle seemed to pass—not from either of them, but from the other end of the line. If Nokia 1100 had eyebrows, they'd have been raised with smug delight. "This is the boy you chose?" it seemed to whisper, its tone teasing, almost proud. Nokia 2280 didn't respond. It had grown used to him by now—his silences, his delays, his strange way of understanding love a few moments too late. It just blinked softly, as if to say, "He's slow… but he's mine."

And in a quiet corner of the kitchen, still snug inside its jar, the Bournvita sat untouched—but not unfeeling. If jars could smile, this one would've.

The Nokia 2280 lay close to him. It felt the warmth of his palm, the quiet joy that had settled in his breath, and for the first time in many days, it rested without worry. Everything it had carried—every hesitation, every unsent word—had finally reached where it was meant to.

Then came a soft buzz. A message. The screen lit up again. And just like that, the unease returned. What if she had changed her mind? What if the call had been a mistake—a slip of the heart she had now thought better of? What if… it was Girish after all?

The phone waited, tense in its silence, watching as his eyes moved across the screen. A faint smile broke on his lips—quiet, involuntary. He leaned back, exhaled, and this time, the sigh carried no weight. Just contentment.

From: Aparna

I told you I like Tax Planners!!! Happy Valentine's Day, my free tax advisor and financial expert!

He chuckled softly and typed back without overthinking:

Happy Valentine's Day, my Home Minister.

Then paused.

His thumb hovered over the screen for a second too long.

Backspace, backspace, backspace.

He deleted the words my Home Minister — leaving just:

Happy Valentine's Day.

The phone blinked gently. So, this had been her plan. To wait for the day when hearts are most often spoken for. It would've smiled, if it knew how.

Pranav had already fallen asleep—his breathing calm, his hand resting near the phone, as if ready for another day to begin.

CHAPTER 27

The next station is Saket. The doors will open on the right. Please mind the gap.

The voice crackled through the Delhi metro coach, calm and indifferent, as if it hadn't just interrupted something that had taken months to say.

Outside, Delhi blurred into itself—dusty trees, long stretches of flyovers, rows of silent apartments. Inside, the air carried a strange kind of stillness, the kind that doesn't ask for attention but is always noticed.

On one of the side seats, two people sat in silence.

Pranav leaned slightly forward, elbows on his knees, his eyes resting somewhere in the middle distance. He had been speaking for a while now. Not in a rush. Not with drama. Just words placed gently into the air—like stones dropped into a quiet lake.

Beside him sat Mallika. His colleague. She worked in Administration; he was with Accounts. They were part of a small bilateral organisation in Gurgaon (Now Gurugram)—just a handful of employees, the kind of place where formalities were few, and conversations often carried over from work to the shared auto stand. They weren't particularly close. But sometimes, in offices that small, all it took was time for people to grow familiar.

It had taken him months to speak of it—since that quiet February night when the message was sent.

And yet, once he began, the words had come easily. As if they'd been waiting—not just to be said, but to be heard.

Mallika didn't speak immediately. But there was a glint in her eyes that hadn't been there a few minutes ago. She looked at him—not with pity, not even with surprise—but with a strange, bubbling energy, the kind that comes when someone realises they've just lost a quiet competition they didn't know they were part of. For the past few weeks, she had believed her story was the most interesting, the most emotional, the most deserving of attention. But now… this? This was something else.

She turned to him, half-smiling, as if trying to cover up something she herself hadn't expected to feel. "Yours is a Bollywood-style movie, Pranav," she said, nudging him lightly with her elbow. "So, what happened next?" Her voice carried a mock seriousness, but her eyes gave her away—they were shining with the kind of curiosity that only comes when one story begins to quietly outshine another.

"We haven't spoken since May," he said quietly, his voice softer than before. For a moment, even the metro seemed to slow down—just enough to make one wonder if it too had leaned in to listen. The rhythm of the train steadied, but something in his tone lingered in the air, like a sentence left unfinished.

He looked down, as if the answer was somewhere between the floor and his own thoughts. "It was my mistake," he added, almost as if he was telling that to himself more than to her. "The next station is Green Park. The doors will open on the right."

The announcement came again, but this time, the metro itself seemed to hesitate—as if, for a fleeting moment, it had tried its best to slow down, to linger just a little longer. After all, it had been a quiet witness to a story not found in books or movies, a love story gently unravelled between stations and silences.

Mallika stood up. Her expression had changed. She looked at him with something between a smile and concern—light-hearted, but not indifferent. "Bye, Pranav. We'll talk again. And don't worry… fights do happen. Sometimes, distance is needed too."

She didn't wait for a reply. She stepped out just as the doors opened, leaving behind a soft trace of jasmine and a quiet sense of something unfinished—not a goodbye, but the promise of a next chapter.

A part of her already knew: the story wasn't over. And tomorrow, she would return—not just to hear the rest, but perhaps, in her own quiet way, to help bring it to where it was always meant to end

Pranav got off a few stations later, lost in thought. As the doors closed behind him, the metro seemed to sigh softly, as if hoping—perhaps foolishly—that it might be lucky enough to hear the rest of the story someday. After all, not every journey came with such silence, such truth.

By the time he reached home, the house was quiet again. Dinner was simple—routine, even—but the weight of that one sentence still echoed in his mind: It was my mistake. He didn't try to distract himself. Instead, he opened the drawer, pulled out a brown-coloured diary—old, ordinary, but somehow heavier tonight. It had waited long enough.

And now, what had lived inside him for months was finally ready to come out.

CHAPTER 28

The night didn't feel heavy, but it had a certain stillness—the kind that settles in only when everything else has already been said.

The ceiling fan turned in slow, predictable circles. A bedsheet, folded at the foot of the bed, held the shape of a crease that hadn't been pressed out. The window was half open—not for air, but because no one had remembered to close it. Even the clock ticked with an unhurried rhythm, as if it too had agreed to move a little slower tonight.

Pranav sat on the edge of the bed, neither stiff nor relaxed—just still. His legs were drawn in loosely, one hand resting over the other, as if holding onto nothing in particular. For a long time, he didn't move. He didn't need to. The silence around him didn't ask for answers—only presence.

The Nokia 2280 lay beside him, silent and still. Its screen remained dark, though it had more to say than it ever did when it lit up. For once, it chose not to blink, not to buzz, and most of all—not to reveal what it already knew.

The diary lay in front of him on the bed, a few inches from where he sat. Its cover was slightly arched from years of use. It didn't move, didn't call out—but it held his gaze the way unfinished conversations often do. It had carried the truth for long enough. Tonight, it seemed ready to let it unfold—quietly, on its own terms.

For a while, he didn't move. The diary stayed where it was, and so did he.

And then, with a breath that wasn't quite deep but needed to be, he reached out.

The fingers that had hesitated all evening now pressed gently against the corner of the cover. The first page lifted—no creak, no rustle. Just a slow motion, as if even the paper knew it was time.

From the half-open window, a breeze entered the room—not strong, but certain. It passed through the curtain, touched the edge of the page, and continued its way across the room, carrying something that hadn't yet been spoken.

The page settled without a sound. And just beyond the words, something long left behind began to return—quietly, as if it had never really gone.

And just like that, a familiar train coach returned—she was already seated by the window, chin on palm, eyes lost in the platform's fading rhythm. Her name on the reservation chart had made him pause, but she hadn't recognised him. Not yet. A few unsure words followed, a playful challenge set between them: if he could remind her who he was, she'd give him her number—maybe even coffee. If he failed, no more talking till Lucknow. So, he began. Shared summers, a guava tree, terrace cricket, the red house in Mehndi Tola. Her expression shifted slowly. Then suddenly— "Manu!" she had laughed, and the coach had turned to look. One man stood, questioning. She answered softly, without hesitation: "He's my childhood friend. We're meeting after twelve years." That was all. Later, near the auto stand, she slipped him her number with a smile that didn't need context. The coffee never happened. But something else had already begun.

The page turned, and with it returned a quiet evening. The messages hadn't changed—light, teasing, familiar—but something in his words had begun to ask for more. He had told her, simply, that life felt better with her in it. And she, half-joking, half-deflecting, had wondered aloud why everyone kept proposing to her. He smiled then, even typed back a joke—called her a marriage product. But beneath the laughter, the silence grew. Why do we have to complicate relationships, Pranav? she had asked. He didn't know. Only that he was a boy who had fallen for a friend. That wasn't a crime. But maybe it was a risk. Still, that night, the phone lay glowing beside him—waiting. And so did he

A faint silence settled between the lines, as if even the diary needed a moment to breathe. The page turned—not loudly, not deliberately. Just enough to let something new begin.

The message had been sent, but understanding took its time. When her voice finally came, it carried caution, clarity, and a softness that didn't need explanation. She spoke of Girish, of careers, of things not ready—but somewhere in between, she said it: after his CA, after her posting, she'd talk to her parents. And they would say yes. That was it. A yes disguised in future plans, wrapped in calm certainty. But the boy who had waited so long didn't quite catch it. He asked if she was rejecting him. The phone nearly sighed. She didn't. Instead, she laughed—light, scolding, unmistakably hers— "Aree buddhu… itna bhi nahi samjhe?" That was her answer. Not in words, but in tone, in laughter, in a promise that had already been made. And for once, even the silence between them smiled.

The room had grown quiet again, but not the peaceful kind. The kind that arrives when something unspoken lingers too long. The bed, which had held him so steadily until now, felt the shift— his weight no longer even, his presence less still. A soft creak escaped the mattress, as if it, too, sensed what the next page might carry. The fingers hovered, uncertain. And then, despite the body's quiet protest, the page turned.

It had begun with a Facebook request. She had sent it, and he had accepted—something so simple, and yet, in hindsight, perhaps the first step into a mistake he hadn't understood at the time. One by one, her friends appeared on his screen. He added them too. The chats were casual, polite, nothing unusual. But slowly, unknowingly, he had crossed a line. What felt harmless to him may have seemed careless to her—or worse, intrusive. And he hadn't stopped. That was the part that stayed with him. He had stepped too far into a world that hadn't invited him in.

Not out of malice.

Another page turned, slower than before. The paper didn't resist, but it didn't welcome the touch either—as if it knew what lay ahead, and wasn't eager to revisit it.

He had forgotten what she'd once said—that she rarely picked up calls. It wasn't new. She had always been that way. But back then, he didn't remember. Or maybe he didn't want to. The calls kept increasing, one after another, most of them unanswered. Each ring felt longer than it was. And with every silence on the other end, something inside him tightened. He wasn't angry. Just afraid. What if she stopped replying altogether? What if this ended the same way the last one did? The thought of another silence—one like Trapta's—shook him more than he let on. So he called again. And again. As if foolishness could somehow fix what fear had already begun to break.

The next page didn't turn easily. It clung to the one before it, as if even paper hesitated to relive what came next. But the hand moved anyway. Slowly. Quietly. The truth was still waiting

The calls had stopped, but the messages hadn't. Facebook became the next refuge—one message after another, all left unanswered. At first, they were simple: just checking in, just wondering. But they grew. Without planning to, he had started filling the silences with words she hadn't asked for. It wasn't love anymore—it was fear in disguise. Fear that if he stayed quiet, she'd forget him. That she'd move on, like others had. So, he typed. Long after she'd stopped replying. Long after silence had become the answer. Looking back now, he knew it wasn't just a mistake. It was a blunder. The kind that doesn't shout its wrongness in the moment—but lingers, quietly, in regret.

The page turned—hesitant, reluctant, like a curtain being drawn over something no one wanted to see. He didn't know when it all began to fall apart. Or why. Or how. Just that it did. Slowly at first, like a crack forming beneath the surface. Then all at once. One day, her message came—short, final, and unlike anything before. A line that didn't ask for understanding. It simply said what it had to. And that was it.

Everything stood still. The breeze outside, which had been rustling the curtain softly a moment ago, paused mid-air—as if unsure whether to enter. The light from the room dimmed slightly, not because of a power cut, but as if the bulb itself no longer wished to witness what was coming. Beside him, the Nokia 2280 lay in its usual place—but not usual at all. That day, it had tried. Tried to hold the message back. It even reached out, in its own silent way, to Nokia 1100—pleading through unseen signals: "Please… ask her to stop. He's not like that." But Nokia 1100, ever loyal to its owner, remained quiet. Or perhaps it had already known what was about to be sent. And then, the screen blinked. A message delivered. That was the day Nokia 2280 cried. Or would have, if it knew how. And quietly, without protest, it showed the message.

There were no explanations. Just words that appeared on the screen—measured, distant, and final.

I don't want to stay in touch. I don't want to feel embarrassed because of any friend in my life. Please, stop entering my personal space like this. And please... don't call again. Goodbye.

That was the last message.

Goodbye.......The girl who had always ended every conversation with 'See you later' had said 'Goodbye.'

Maybe she hadn't meant to sound so distant. Maybe her fingers had paused over the keys too, unsure of whether to press send. It wasn't easy to say goodbye. Not for someone who had once said 'See you later' like it was second nature. Perhaps it had hurt her too. But by then, his mistakes had piled up like unanswered messages—too many to ignore, too much to carry forward. And maybe, just maybe, she had run out of patience long before she ran out of kindness

And that thought—that maybe she too had felt something— only made the truth harder to bear.

And in that moment, he knew—this wasn't just a mistake.

It was a blunder.

The screen dimmed again, but the words stayed. They echoed longer than most memories ever do. A moment passed. And then, the page turned—not quickly, not with purpose, but the way one turns a page they wish they didn't have to read.

What could he have done? He had never truly known the language of friendship. Especially not the kind that stayed. Especially not with girls. None had lasted. Some had smiled and disappeared. Others had been kind but never stayed long enough to be called friends. He often wondered if the idea of having even one female friend was simply not meant for him.

And then came Aparna. The one who never asked much but gave more than anyone ever had. It had felt like a gift. Like something he wasn't supposed to have, but somehow did. And maybe that was the problem. He spoke too soon. Should have waited—two years, like she had said. Maybe they were meant to end up together. But he ruined it. And now, he wasn't sure what he had lost more: a friend, or the only person who had ever truly understood him.

Just as that thought settled—

The screen of the Nokia 2280 lit up—sudden and bright, almost too loud for a night that had gone completely still. The Nokia 2280 hadn't meant to interrupt. Not when he was lost inside pages, he hadn't turned in months. For a moment, it almost felt guilty—like a friend who speaks out of turn, unsure if they've broken something sacred. But then again… maybe that's what friends are for. To pull you out, gently, when you're slipping too deep.

He picked up the phone, slower this time—his eyes still heavy, his thumb unsure.

Her message wasn't dramatic. It didn't pretend to fix anything. But somehow, it held the quiet steadiness he needed in that moment.

I'll pray and I'll do whatever I can to help sort things between you and Aparna.

Then a pause. And one last line.

But tomorrow, you have to tell me everything. Good night.

Pranav didn't respond. Not right away. The phone rested quietly in his hand, but his thoughts had already drifted. Inside his mind, something moved—trying to name what he had lost.

A best friend? No… not quite. A great friend? Closer, but still not enough. A special friend. That's what she had been. The only one. And if Mallika could somehow bring her back—not in the way people expect, but even as a friend—he didn't know how. But if she did, he would always be grateful. Marriage or no marriage, he just wanted one female friend who stayed.

His gaze fell back on the diary, now lying open beside him.

He wasn't reading it anymore.

He was watching himself inside it—quietly, painfully, page by page.

CHAPTER 29

The next morning, when Mallika walked into the office, something about her seemed out of place. Her hair was loosely tied, her black top looked crumpled and faded, and her blue jeans bore the signs of yesterday's wear. Her eyes were swollen, red at the edges, as though sleep had forgotten her doorstep. Even the faint fragrance that usually lingered around her was missing, as if she had left it behind in a hurry—or perhaps, forgotten it altogether.

Pranav stood by the corner desk, adjusting the files that didn't need adjusting. He glanced up as Mallika walked in. Her steps were slower than usual, her gaze fixed somewhere near the floor.

"Good morning," he said, his voice careful. "You're looking beautiful today."

Mallika didn't stop. She brushed past him with a faint nod. "Morning. No jokes, please," she murmured, as if the words were meant more for herself than for him.

He followed her with his eyes, then added softly, "You know… no one ever tries to decorate a rainbow. It's just there—beautiful on its own."

She halted, only for a second. Her hand tightened around the strap of her handbag. Then she turned, slowly, her face unreadable.

"I know what you're trying to do," she said, her tone steady, stripped of emotion. "But this won't work. Kindness doesn't undo everything. "Do you really think you can persuade me to reconsider my relationship with Sourav?"

But even as she said it, a part of her was already thinking of Sourav.

There was a time when Mallika spoke of Sourav as if he had stepped out of a romantic film—thoughtful, composed, and full of quiet gestures that made the ordinary feel special. They had met at a college seminar on modern poetry. He was late, apologised over spilled coffee, and smiled in a way that softened the chaos. What followed was a long walk-through quiet lane and two forgotten cups of cold coffee—something she would later describe, half-laughing, as a scene borrowed from an old Shah Rukh Khan film.

Sourav had a calm presence and a thoughtful way of speaking. He listened without interrupting, spoke of poetry as if it were personal, and always remembered the little things. Mallika used to believe she had found what others only searched for.

But something had shifted during that metro ride with Pranav the previous evening. She hadn't meant to feel anything at all—she had only planned to listen. And yet, as he spoke—quietly, awkwardly, with the weight of years pressing on each sentence—it left her unsettled. Not because she felt drawn to him, but because something in his story made her wonder if she truly understood what love was supposed to feel like.

That night, long after the metro ride and long after they had gone their separate ways, Pranav sat with his diary open in his lap. He was reading a page he had once written but never shown to anyone—a confession wrapped in hesitation and lined with regret. As he traced the lines with his finger, something inside him sank—not because of what he had written, but because he knew it had taken him too long to admit it. His phone buzzed softly beside him.

Pranav… this is Mallika. It's about Sourav. I don't know how to explain it, but something doesn't feel the same anymore. I want to step away from this relationship.

Just the day before, Mallika had believed she would help Pranav find his way back to Aparna. Now, it was her own relationship that stood uncertain—quietly shifting, not from anger or conflict, but from something even harder to explain: clarity.

He didn't respond immediately. For a moment, he simply looked at her—calm, composed, almost amused. Then, with a quiet smile and a steady voice, he said confidently,

"Of course I can."

She didn't look away.

"Pranav," she said, her voice calm but carrying the weight of something final, "I've already told you... I don't want to continue with Sourav."

There was a brief silence—just enough to let the words settle.

"I've ended that relationship," she added, her tone firmer now, as if repeating it made it more real. "It's done."

She inhaled slowly, blinked once, and then said—softer this time, but with unmistakable clarity, "If you really consider me your friend... then please... let me be. For some time."

Her eyes widened—not in anger, but in the way people do when they're holding back more than they're ready to share.

There was a pause—long enough for the distant click of a keyboard and the muted shuffle of paper to fill the silence. She didn't say anything, just looked away, her fingers tracing the edge of the table without purpose.

Sensing the moment, Pranav spoke—not forcefully, but with the quiet steadiness of someone who had been holding back.

"I can't see my friend like this," he said softly. "You're hurting, even if you won't admit it."

He waited a moment before continuing.

"I still remember the way you used to talk about Sourav… that walk after the poetry seminar, the coffee neither of you finished, the way you smiled when you told me how he remembered your mother's favourite mithai without being told."

Her eyes didn't meet his, but she had stopped fidgeting.

"I don't know what happened between you," he said, "but I do know this—Sourav's life will be blank without your presence. He loves you. And whatever it was… I believe he regrets it."

He looked down at his hands, then said quietly, "Just call him once. That's all."

There was a pause.

Mallika slowly lifted her hand—perhaps to adjust her hair, perhaps for something else—but Pranav's cheeks tensed immediately, as if they had taken a decision of their own. A quiet panic bloomed across his face, like a student who'd given the wrong answer and was waiting for the chalk to fly.

But she didn't say a word about it.

She simply stood up, looked at him calmly, and said, "Let me go to the washroom, cry a little bit more, and then I'll come back after washing my face."

His face softened, though not entirely. The computer screen dimmed politely, as if trying to pretend it hadn't seen anything at all.

A few minutes later, Mallika stepped out of the washroom—and it was as if a different person had returned. The kohl was back, the light fragrance returned, and despite the unironed top, she carried herself like a bride walking into her own reception.

She stood in front of Pranav and smiled.

"Thank you, Pranav," she said. "How do I look? Beautiful, no? Ignore the wrinkles on the top—I remember what you said. No one decorates a rainbow."

She adjusted her hair with a practiced flick and added, almost like an afterthought, "Everything's fine now. We'll be having lunch together today. Please… handle the situation."

Pranav opened his mouth, but no words arrived. The printer whirred to life in the corner, as if it too had been caught off guard by this sudden change

The director of the organisation was away on an official tour, but the office hadn't gone lax. It never did. Divided by a glass wall, the scientific and administration & accounts departments sat side by side—close enough to share glances, yet far enough to pretend not to notice each other.

Mallika worked in the administration department—two cabins, six compact workstations, and just enough space for whispers to travel undetected. Her seat wasn't far from Ms. Lalitha's cabin, and while the door remained open, her gaze rarely strayed from the glass.

Ms. Lalitha, Scientific Officer, mid-forties, sat in her usual corner—half in shadow, half in command. Though the director's chair was empty, her presence filled the void with silent authority. She didn't need to speak. The transparent wall did it for her.

When Mallika casually mentioned lunch, Pranav's hands froze above the keyboard. The words were light, but the room wasn't. Even across the glass, he could feel the shift—Lalitha's head didn't move, but her eyes had.

Pranav didn't respond right away. He glanced sideways, then at the exit register near the door. Everything about this space was polished and quiet—and still, sending Mallika out for lunch felt like walking barefoot in a room full of glass.

The office—new as it was—seemed to notice. The partitions listened. The chairs leaned. And somewhere between a file being closed and a drawer sliding shut, the atmosphere filed its own report.

There was a pause—brief, but enough for the moment to feel longer than it was. Mallika didn't say anything. Her fingers adjusted the corner of a paper she had already straightened twice. Her smile lingered, but her eyes carried the faint nervousness of someone who had just taken a bold step.

Pranav sat still, unsure whether to look at her or look away.

Then, leaning in slightly, he whispered, "Mallika... how will I manage Ms. Lolitha?"

(The name—more of a nickname than a title—had been given by Pankaj, equal parts fear and humour.)

Mallika turned, her expression shifting back to that familiar mix of charm and mischief. "Please, Pranav," she said, soft but dramatic. "Think of something. You're so smart. You can do anything. You're a... a magician. Won't you help your friend?"

Her eyes, lit by innocence and lined with kohl, carried more than what she said. Those lashes—artful and perfectly placed—fluttered once, and in that one moment, Pranav felt his heartbeat stammer. It wasn't just flattery. It was surrender, in disguise.

"With that kind of flattery," he thought, "anyone would have agreed."

He gave a half-smile. "Alright. Let me think. I'll work out a plan to get past Madam Lolitha. Don't worry… you'll have your lunch with your would-be hus…"

He didn't finish. The moment had already completed the sentence.

Mallika looked at him for a moment longer than usual. Her voice dropped just a little—still steady, but with a softness that hadn't been there a minute ago.

"Thank you," she said. "You're a true friend."

Then, with the faintest smile tugging at the corner of her lips, she added, "I'll pray… that everything sorts itself out between you and Aparna."

She didn't wait for a reply. She just let the words hang in the air, light but lingering.

Pranav gave her a long, tired look.

"If you're quite done making me a saint," he said, "I'd like a moment to think."

He shifted the papers on his desk—not because he needed to, but because it gave him something to do with his hands.

"You get back to work," Pranav said, straightening a file that didn't need straightening. "You've already wasted enough time today."

For a split second, he braced himself—for the usual glare, maybe even a sharp retort.

But none came.

Mallika gave a small nod—quiet, obedient, almost too obedient. Then, with mock seriousness, she raised her hand in salute.

"Aye aye, Captain," she said, and turned to her screen.

Her fingers began moving over the keyboard—slow at first, then picking up pace. She even muttered something about formatting errors, just loud enough for him to hear.

(And yes—she was actually working. Not pretending. Definitely not pretending. Because if Mallika ever reads this… well, the narrator would very much prefer to keep his spine intact.)

Pranav ji… today again?" Pankaj said at last, his voice calm, almost amused.

He had been listening the whole time, without a word. But now, with his chin resting on one hand and his eyes barely leaving his screen, he glanced over—just long enough to make his point.

The kind of glance that didn't ask for an answer. It already knew one.

Mallika sat with her earplugs in, head tilted slightly. Her fingers moved across the keyboard with quiet rhythm. Every now and then, she nodded faintly—just enough to suggest a song was playing in. The cursor blinked steadily on the screen, waiting for a response that wasn't coming.

Pranav sat at his desk, pretending to read an email he had already read twice. A file lay open beside him, untouched. From somewhere in the distance, a chair creaked, followed by the soft clink of someone closing a tiffin box too early.

He glanced at the corner of his screen but quickly looked away—as if acknowledging the time would only add pressure to the quiet failure building inside his head.

There was still no plan.

His fingers hovered over the keyboard, then dropped to his lap. He let out a slow breath—the kind that came not from tiredness, but from quiet resignation.

There was something about men—especially the well-behaved ones in offices. They could refuse meetings, delay reports, even skip meals… but they couldn't say no to a colleague who smiled at them with hopeful eyes and wore confidence like perfume.

And Pranav, despite all his good sense and grey cells, was no exception.

He wasn't thinking about deadlines. Not anymore. He was thinking about a lunch plan. For someone else.

And like many well-meaning fools before him, he was doing it for a girl who had done nothing more than smile, flutter her lashes, and ask for help as if he were the only one in the world who could give it.

Just as he was deep in thought—still without a plan—the intercom rang.

It was Ms. Lolitha. She wanted to see both Pankaj and him in her cabin.

By the time they reached the door, Pankaj had already adjusted his collar. Pranav tapped gently on the glass and waited.

"Good afternoon, madam. May we come in?"

"Afternoon," she said, without looking up. "Yes, you may. Please have a seat."

They sat.

And then it began.

The voice was even, slow, and stretched out like a lecture given in a warm room after lunch. Somewhere between "quarterly reconciliation" and "pending clarifications," Pranav felt his attention slipping.

She spoke of administrative reports, financial summaries, compliance notes, and something about stock registers—but the words started melting into each other.

He nodded occasionally, just to appear alive.

It wasn't that he didn't understand. He did. But some voices had the power to make even urgency sound like bedtime.

Ms. Lolitha adjusted her spectacles, her eyes narrowing with the kind of focus usually reserved for forensic inspectors. She began going through the papers, one by one—silently at first, then with a faint tightening of her lips.

"Can you please explain this?" she said, pointing at a column in the petty cash register.

Pankaj cleared his throat. "Madam, that's the petty cash register. These are routine disbursals—small expenses."

He had barely finished the sentence when she turned the page and said, "Leave that. What about the administrative advance from last quarter?"

It was always like this.

In the director's absence, Ms. Lolitha assumed the chair—if not physically, then certainly in spirit. And once seated, she rarely stayed on one topic long enough for the other person to catch up.

Her questions had the habit of travelling faster than answers could be formed. No one ever quite knew what was coming next.

"Pranav, what about the stationery that was supposed to be delivered today—for the upcoming meeting?"

There was a moment of silence. Pankaj let out a slow, silent breath—almost relieved that the storm had moved past him. Pranav, seated beside him, straightened his back just slightly, sensing the shift in direction.

Oh! How could he have forgotten that?

Pranav turned slightly and looked at Pankaj, whose lips had already curled into a devilish smile. It said everything without needing to move.

For the first time, he felt like thanking Ms. Lolitha. She had unknowingly handed him a brilliant idea. The stationery!

Finally, there was a way to send Mallika out—without raising any alarms.

"Madam," he said, clearing his throat with practiced formality, "we could ask Mallika to visit the supplier—to check the status of our stationery order. And since she..."

"Madam," Pankaj added, cutting in at just the right moment, "she also hasn't brought her lunch today."

Ms. Lolitha didn't blink. She simply nodded, as though approving an inventory request.

"Well then, she'll have to leave now so that she's back by 2:30," she said.

Ms. Lolitha flipped through a file, her finger landing on the top entry. She glanced up briefly, then picked up the receiver and dialled Mallika's extension. Her voice was calm, procedural, and carried no trace of generosity.

A few minutes later, Mallika walked in. She stood with her hands behind her back, listening.

A short instruction was delivered—pointed, measured, unmistakably final.

Mallika nodded. Once. Then again. She turned and stepped back, her pace steady, her expression unreadable.

Pankaj rose almost too quickly, adjusting his chair with unnecessary care. Pranav followed, collecting his papers like a man who had just been granted a rare pardon.

They stepped out of the cabin with quiet obedience.

The office noticed.

The glass partition gave a faint creak. A chair adjusted itself as if finally breathing. Even the ceiling fan spun a little smoother—still pretending not to care, but clearly relieved at the silence that followed.

Mallika returned to her seat, slipped her earplugs back in, and continued typing—for appearance, mostly. Her eyes flicked once toward Pranav, and when no one was looking, she leaned ever so slightly in his direction.

"You really are a wizard," she whispered. "I knew you'd find a way. Thanks, buddy."

Pranav didn't look at her. He kept his eyes on the screen and replied quietly, "Shh… now go. And don't forget to visit the stationers."

It was what Ms. Lolitha had said, word for word—Mallika would check the status of the stationery order at HKV Stationers, be allowed to have lunch outside, and be back by 2:30. No wandering.

Mallika gave a small nod, opened a drawer, and began collecting her things. The glow on her face was hard to miss, even in the soft office light.

Mallika left the room with her usual grace, though her steps had a certain lightness they didn't carry on ordinary days. Her earrings swayed ever so slightly, as if they too were in on the secret.

Pankaj, still at his workstation, leaned toward Pranav once she was out of sight. He asked—half serious, half smiling—whether Pranav truly believed she would check on the stationery order.

Pranav didn't answer immediately. He adjusted his chair, looked briefly at the office clock, then toward the glass door that had just closed behind her. With the faintest smirk, he muttered something about divine intervention being the only authority on that matter.

Pankaj let out a quiet chuckle and returned to his screen.

A printer somewhere resumed its duties with a hesitant hum, as if registering its quiet doubt too. The rollers slowed midway through a page—paused—then resumed with a resigned clatter, as though accepting that whatever came next was out of its hands. If it could sigh, it might have.

Mallika returned back on time—only if one was willing to stretch the lunch break by half an hour.

She walked in with a face that gave away more than she realised. Her eyes were brighter. Her walk had a rhythm. And the soft smile on her lips, though quickly tucked away, lingered just long enough to say something had gone exactly as she hoped.

She sat down in front of her computer, adjusted the chair slightly, and exhaled with a kind of happiness that didn't need explaining.

If she owed Pranav anything, she didn't say it. But the way she looked at her screen—then, briefly, in his direction—said enough.

A few minutes later, Mallika appeared at Pranav's desk— breathless, wide-eyed, and clearly not at peace with the world.

Her voice trembled, and her hands wouldn't stay still. She said something about being in trouble, needing help, and how only Pranav could save her from certain doom.

Pankaj looked up from his monitor and asked what had happened now.

Before she could answer, Pranav gently stepped in. He explained, in that calm tone office veterans usually reserve for fire drills, that Mallika had forgotten to bring the order status from the stationers.

Mallika turned to Pankaj, gesturing dramatically—like someone falsely accused. She insisted that Pranav could read minds, and begged him to protect her just one last time. Her tone held the kind of innocence that came with wide eyes and unshakable belief in male foolishness.

Pranav didn't respond with words. He simply told her to check her drawer.

She did.

Inside, neatly placed, was the printed email—a proforma invoice from HKV Stationers, with order details, status, and delivery date.

Pranav and Pankaj didn't exchange a word. But the silence between them said: they knew she'd forget. And so, like every other idiot before them, they had called the stationers themselves and requested the document in advance.

Somewhere in the universe, another report on gender behaviour could've been filed.

Mallika exhaled visibly. She took the paper, smoothed it out, and walked straight to Ms. Lolitha's cabin—relieved, rescued, and once again, undefeated.

It was four o'clock when Ms. Lolitha finally left for the day. Before leaving, she issued instructions the way a major might brief a battalion—stern, sharp, and with no room for misinterpretation. They nodded in sync, knowing there was no escape before six. But the moment the door shut behind her, the air in the room loosened. The office, though unchanged in size, suddenly felt roomier.

Not long after, Mallika appeared beside Pranav's desk again. There was no mischief in her eyes this time—just a strange sort of warmth, as if something had settled within her.

She said something about him being a rare kind of friend. One with a golden heart. Something about how he could have taken advantage of her vulnerable moment—how she would have accepted it too, perhaps even welcomed it. But instead, he had helped her hold together what mattered.

And now, what mattered was still there—because of him.

Pranav said nothing. He smiled, gently. But the more she spoke, the more that smile seemed to tighten—like a thread pulled slightly too far.

She continued. Wondered aloud how someone like him could go through life without a single female friend. How Aparna, of all people, had failed to see what was so plainly visible. She said she believed things would work out. That some people walk away too quickly, only to realise what they left behind.

And just as she said it, his phone rang.

It was a soft sound—nothing urgent about it—but something in it made him reach for it right away. He took it out, glanced at the screen… and paused.

Mallika leaned in out of habit, and before he could tilt the screen away, she had already seen the name.

Aparna.

She didn't squeal. Didn't clap. But her body said everything. Her eyes widened, and her hand flew to her mouth in the kind of gesture people make when they've seen a prophecy fulfilled. Her excitement filled the air like scent—sweet, bright, and completely uncontained.

She looked at him as if to say, See? I told you so. She's calling to make things right. My intuitions never lie. She's back.

Then she lifted her hand again, as if nudging an invisible curtain between them, her eyes narrowing just enough to say, "Pick it up, you fool."

Pranav met her gaze, then spoke quietly—barely louder than the hum of the fan above.

"Don't shout. I'm answering."

Mallika then glanced at his face—not with suspicion, but with the cautious curiosity one reserves for people who say strange things with a straight face.

She was searching for something—relief, joy, even the hint of a smile.

But Pranav gave her nothing. His face remained still, calm, unreadable.

And in his hand, the Nokia 2280 rested quietly. Its screen glowed, casting a faint light across his fingers—as if it too was waiting, unsure of what would happen next.

ABOUT THE AUTHOR

CA Pranav Sharma

Pranav Sharma is a Chartered Accountant who never imagined he would one day write a novel. What began as a quiet feeling stayed with him—growing gently, patiently, until it found its voice in these pages. He doesn't consider himself a writer, just someone who had something to say. This is his first step into storytelling, and if the words stayed with you… that's all he ever hoped for

Email: capranav.author@gmail.com
Facebook: www.facebook.com/pranav.author
Instagram: @capranav_author
Website: www.capranavauthor.com